The PROPERER MAN

The PROPERER MAN

BETH FUCHS

This is a work of fiction. Names, characters, business, events and incidents are the products of the author's imagination. Any resemblance to actual persons, living or dead, or actual events is purely coincidental.

Printed in the United States of America
ISBN 978-1-641336-56-7 (hc)
ISBN 978-1-947352-22-3 (sc)
ISBN 978-1-641336-57-4 (e)

Library of Congress Control Number: 2021916558

Romance/Fiction
09.11.2021

MainSpring Books
5901 W. Century Blvd
Suite 750
Los Angeles, CA, US, 90045

www.mainspringbooks.com

For almost thirty years, I have taught Shakespeare's Romeo and Juliet *to ninth graders. Sheer repetition has enhanced my interpretation of this famous tragedy. I have come to realize Friar Laurence is, despite his good intentions, an unethical opportunist, trying to garner the Prince's attention by positioning himself to be the one who receives credit for ending the Capulet-Montague feud. Rather than being a wise advisor, the friar resorts to deceiving a family into believing their only child is dead, and then makes the cowardly and unconscionable choice to leave a vulnerable teenager alone in a tomb with the dead body of her first love. Romeo speaks in the hackneyed clichés of a second-rate poet, always in lust, but never in love. And Juliet? She would have been infinitely happier—not to mention alive—had she married Count Paris, who is so persistent in his requests to marry her, and so distraught by her passing, that he intends to come to the churchyard each night and strew her grave with flowers.*

Intrigued by the last notion in particular, I began to write a different version of Shakespeare's well-known play. Just as audiences can enjoy Shakespeare's tragedy of Romeo and Juliet *without having read the poem that inspired the bard—*Arthur Brooke's Tragical History of Romeus and Juliet—*I want readers unfamiliar with "Two households, both alike in dignity" to still enjoy* A Properer Man. *But for those who know the play, I hope you will find delight in locating the allusions, the embedded words and phrases of Shakespeare's oft-quoted work and appreciate this additional layer of meaning.*

The Properer Man

Read o'er the volume of young Paris' face
And find delight writ there with beauty's pen;
Examine every several lineament,
And see how one another lends content;

Romeo and Juliet Act One, Scene Three, Lines 82-85

I anger her sometimes and tell her that Paris is the properer man

Romeo and Juliet Act Two, Scene Four, Lines 177-178

A gentleman of princely parentage,
Of fair desmesnes, youthful, and nobly trained
Stuffed, as they say, with honorable parts,
Proportioned as one's thoughts would wish a man

Romeo and Juliet Act Three, Scene Five, Lines 180-183

O, he's a lovely gentleman! Romeo's a dishclout to him.

Romeo and Juliet Act Three, Scene Five, Lines 220-221

ONE

*R*OME *AYO, THE POP SUPER STAR* who won the Best Album Grammy Award *last year for* Cold Fire, *was found dead late this morning. His death was reported by the owner of* The Vault, *an exclusive New York City nightspot that caters to celebrities. Ayo was found in the bathroom of one the club's suites where he was pronounced dead on the scene. Police Chief, Captain Trey Watchman, has ruled out foul play and found no evidence to suggest suicide. A preliminary autopsy indicated extreme hyperthermia was the cause of death.*

"We are shocked and deeply saddened by Mr. Ayo's untimely death," said Ben Volaire, Ayo's agent and publicist. "I considered him a close friend and a great talent."

Ayo was born in Verona, TN, less than an hour's drive from Nashville, where he embarked on his music career. Even before he graduated from high school, Ayo had joined other aspiring vocal artists, performing in the Music City's karaoke bars, on street corners and other local venues, all with the hopes of being discovered. His first top forty song, "Rosaline" actually appeared on the country charts, but Ayo found the genre "too confining" and quickly crossed over to pop, where his sultry good looks and emotionally-charged live concert performances quickly propelled him to super-stardom. I Am Too Bold *sold over 10 million copies world-wide. Murray Q., music critic for* Rolling Stone, *praised the album for its intensity, playful hyperbole and skillful use of changing rhythms. "Rome Ayo can never again be dismissed as a pretty face that should front a boy-band. He has proven he is, in every sense, a man who is a legitimate contender in the field."*

Ayo, an only child, is preceded in death by his mother, and is survived by his father. While Ayo has often been photographed with beautiful women at his side, Volaire confirmed Ayo was not involved in any long-term relationship. "Lovely ladies inspired Rome, but his only real love was describing the experience."

TWO

Six days later

THE GRAY PRE-DAWN SKY WAS FLECKED with streaks of light as Dr. Shaelyn K. Speare backed out of her driveway, heading east down Dante Road. She always left the house by 5:00 in the morning so that she could avoid traffic and hit most of lights without stopping, making her commute along mainly residential and commercial roads only 45 minutes. She loved how, in June and July, she was able to witness the pink and then gold of first light even before she pulled into her reserved space at Global Health.

Global Health looked nothing like a psychiatric hospital and clinic. It was situated not far from the coast, along a country road lined with multi-million dollar estates. In fact, it had once been a residence built by James Tudor, an entrepreneur who had realized the potential of the internet early on, and, along with his wife Anne, had made a fortune selling retailers' excess stock to a global market. Having created a successful company in the first decade of their marriage, they started their family in the second, and after the birth of their first child, commissioned a 20-room mansion on an expanse of exclusive New Jersey real estate less than two hours from the New York City. Their lavish home would not only cater to the desires of a couple living out the fantasy of the ultimate American Dream; it would also allow them to run their online empire from one of its wings, and thus optimize family time.

Two years later, though, suffering from a severe post-partum depression, Anne drowned their second child, an infant daughter, in one of their mansion's six bathrooms. What legal wrangling had been necessary to transition the Tudor residence to a medical facility was not Shae Speare's bailiwick. She only knew that James Tudor had become a tireless advocate for women's mental health, and had hired her as the senior staff psychiatrist for his mansion-renovated-to-psych-facility. The clientele was limited to women, most well-to-do and overwhelmed with eating disorders, addictions, anxiety, and various sorts of depression. Their high-powered husbands and parents, often discomfited that mental illness did not respect income level, demanded positive, lasting results. Usually, Dr. Speare and her staff delivered. They had earned a sterling reputation for their ability to work through complex problems arising from love, loss, jealousy and guilt.

By arriving early, Dr. Speare could also spend the first couple hours of her day updating case files and reading professional journals before she began meeting with patients at 9:00. But this morning she had left early because she had received a text message from the night nurse, Brooke: *Know u get up early to work out. New patient arrived at 3:30. Attempted suicide. Still sedated.* Dr. Speare liked to be present when such cases woke up; it helped her establish rapport if she could work with them in those first disoriented moments, so she had cut her time on the elliptical short, showered, and left by 4:30. Her husband Andy, whose job at an insurance agency was closer to home and more flexible, was always in charge of waking and getting their twins ready. (Today, Judith had riding lessons, and Hampton would be at soccer camp until 3:00). She would call around 8:00 to make sure their morning was going well.

Once Dr. Speare was on the wooded section of Newman Springs—the least busy stretch of road—she called the direct line to the nurse's station. "Good morning. It's Dr. Shae. I should be there in about a half hour. What's going on with our new admit?"

"She's still out. The EMT's who brought her in said she lost some blood—a cutter—but really there's minimal physical damage. She was sutured in the ER. But there is someone who came down with the ambulance. I'm not sure if it's her boyfriend? Maybe a brother? He wants to talk to you."

"Where is he now?"

"I asked him to wait in the main waiting room since it's self-contained. Prepare yourself. He's drop-dead gorgeous."

"Is that your professional observation?"

"It is the observation of any woman with a pulse."

"I'll judge for myself. See you soon, and start the coffee. It's too early for me to stop."

Other than her Lexus (Tudor had leased it for her. "Are people going to trust their mothers, wives and daughters to a shrink who drives a Chevy Lumina?"), and the familiar cars belonging to the staff, only one other vehicle was parked in the lot: a black Jaguar convertible with New York plates. Dr. Speare's heels clicked along the brick pavement, past the mist of the automatic sprinklers, and paused at the side door, which buzzed once she had swiped her identification badge. She then entered her code to access the entrance into the nurse's station, where Brooke was scanning the screens that monitored all the patients' rooms.

"Hey, Dr. Shae. The coffee's ready."

"Thanks. I'm going to unlock my office, and then I'll go wake up The Hunk."

"I can do it." Far too casual and far too eager at the same time.

"I don't trust you," Dr. Speare winked and picked up the file for the new patient that was already waiting for her in the new admissions tray. "Does the mystery man have a name?

"Conrad Pierce."

Dr. Speare's office consisted of a small waiting area that led to a spacious, book-lined room that, before the renovations, was part of an enormous library. The windows had been converted to block glass for safety and privacy, but they let in enough light so that she could see without turning on any lamps. Still, she switched on her desk light and laid down the file. She looked at her reflection in her computer screen—amused in a self-aware way that she was checking on her appearance just before meeting an alleged contender for a Hollywood leading man. Dabbing beneath her eyes in case her mascara had smudged, Dr. Speare headed across the hall to the waiting room in the still beautiful foyer that was now enclosed in bullet-proof, reinforced glass.

Conrad Pierce was sitting with his head bowed, his cheek resting on his fists, his eyes closed. Perfect dark brown hair, cut cleanly with a natural wave; long lashes; manicured nails; his lean, athletic form clad in such a way he oozed nonchalant sophistication. Brooke's observation was warranted. As soon as Dr. Speare cleared her throat, he shook himself awake, and quickly stood, smiled (as expected, perfect teeth), his hand extended with the automaticity of someone used to greeting others. "Conrad Pierce, but please call me Pierce. When I hear Conrad, I think people are talking to my grandfather."

"So nice to meet you, Pierce." His grip was firm, without being uncomfortable, and the handshake was long enough to be genuine. "Would you like a moment? I can go get us both some coffee and come back for you in a few minutes." Much more discreet than announcing the obvious: that the restroom was in the corner.

"That would be great." When she went to retrieve him and escort him into her office, she could detect the scent of fresh soap. He waited until she asked him to take a seat.

"How do you take your coffee?"

"Black is fine," clearly implying that she need not go to any trouble. "I know I could have just called, but I find that face-to-face meetings are often the most effective."

"In what line of work, Pierce?"

"My family's business. I basically oversee the legal end of things for our insurance division."

Dr. Speare glanced at the clock on her desk. "Of course, at 5:40 in the morning, you're not here to make small talk. What is it that you want to share with me?" The silence lasted long enough to border on becoming awkward, but Dr. Speare was accustomed to such pregnant pauses and knew how to wait.

"Well," Pierce was able to make eye contact only after cursory glance at the book shelves, "when I first got the call that it looked like Julia had tried to commit suicide, I immediately thought of Global. I have a cousin who came here a few years ago when she became bulimic in college. She's doing great now. My mom has mentioned how pleased Aunt Estelle and Uncle Cal were with the treatment she received. So," Pierce brought his open hands together, and this, accompanied by a slight shrug provided closure to his thought.

Dr. Speare smiled before leaning forward to invite the young man's confidence. "We'll do our best for Julia, too. Is this the first time she's done something like this?"

Pierce's expression of genuine confusion was emphasized by his raising his eyebrows before he spoke. "If you had asked me last month if Julia were the type to attempt to kill herself, I would have laughed and asked if you were talking about the right person. I've known her for almost four years, and she is honestly one of the most"—a brief pause as he searched for the right word—"*balanced* people I know. She definitely minimizes her strengths and focuses more on her weaknesses, but that's just the way high-achievers like her are. She's an accurate judge of others' assets and liabilities and is able to accept them. She's private without being secretive or distant. Or at least was." His smile as he uttered the last sentence was cut short as he pressed his lips together to maintain composure.

"And what happened since last month?" Dr. Speare's question was tactfully timed to give Pierce a much-needed moment to reign in his emotions.

"No idea, really. She graduated from Harvard the first week of June. I was there. So were her parents. She seemed happy and was excited about going to work for her dad. We talked that night after I got back into the City; made plans for a weekend at Martha's Vineyard. Then she sent me a text a couple of days later saying she couldn't make it. No explanation. She wouldn't answer my calls, my texts. Of course, when I went to her place in Cambridge, she'd already moved out. She left her parents' penthouse as the forwarding address, but I really don't want to bring them into this if at all possible."

"I noticed the name on the file. Julia's father wouldn't by chance be Loren Cappell?" Pierce nodded to confirm. A real estate titan, Loren "Rich" Cappell had spent one term in the U.S. Senate, evolving into a political celebrity famous for his brash, insulting assessments of politics and policy on Sunday morning talk shows.

"In fact, I would appreciate if you didn't contact the Cappells, at least not yet. If you or Julia think they need to be part of this, I understand. But sometimes Mr. Cappell's reactions can be a little—the hands-together-shrug again before Pierce added diplomatically, "extreme."

Dr. Speare nodded. "My profession is very regulated when it comes to privacy and disclosure, Pierce. I may not be able ethically to reciprocate your candor. I can see, however, that you do care very much for Miss Cappell. Your relationship to her would be?"

Again, pressed lips. The pause. The voice almost controlled as Pierce started to explain. "Last month," another poignant break, "I would have said that I was about to become her fiancé. Now, I don't know."

Dr. Speare stood up, and Pierce took the subtle cue that their conference was over. "I want to be with Julia when she wakes up. Trust me, Pierce, I will do my very best to help her figure out what is going on, and if there is a problem, we'll work through it."

"Thank you, Dr. Speare," Pierce said as he shook Shae's hand again. She noticed his beautiful green eyes were luminous with tears before she escorted him to the waiting area, past the appreciative nurses at their station. After the front door had shut behind him, Shae returned to her office where Pierce's coffee sat untouched on the table beside the armchair where he had been sitting.

THREE

As soon as he was outside, Pierce squeezed his eyes shut until he knew he would not be overwhelmed by an inundation of tears. Then he involuntarily checked his pocket, making sure he had not left his phone behind, and pulled out his keys. He heard the click of the lock and opened the door. Once inside, he took another calming deep breath before punching the address of his office into the GPS. *Acquiring satellites . . . calculating . . . 92 minutes.* Pierce knew at this time of day, rush hour would lengthen that time. He opened his calendar. Nothing really, until 1:00. The adrenaline high of the previous night had faded, and he was aware of the bone-numbing exhaustion that was rushing in to replace it. He entered another search: *Nearby hotels.* He noted the one closest to the Garden State Parkway, west in the direction he'd be going.

Sixteen minutes later, Pierce was standing in a Best Western lobby, explaining to the desk clerk how he had driven in for a meeting in the City and although he'd planned to arrive late last night, the drive had taken far longer than he had estimated. He still wanted some rest. Yes, he understood that he would have to pay for a whole night. Thanks, but he really wasn't interested in the complimentary breakfast being served. "I've set my alarm, but can someone call my room at 10:30 just to make sure I'm up?" A credit card transaction later, he was in a room with a cheap hotel-issued toothbrush and razor. The bed was clean and inviting, and he flopped down on it, kicking off his topsiders.

But instead of sleep, Pierce felt the tears again, thorns pricking behind his eyelids. The images of the blood on the bathroom floor. The hand towel soaked with it. A call to his freshman roommate, Francis, who was now on staff at New York-Presbyterian. Francis had met them at the ER and called Pierce into the examination room three quarters of an hour later. "I gave her a unit of blood. The nurse can tell you how many stitches I needed to close each wrist. Of course, I gave her a tetanus shot and she's sedated." A few questions, and then, "Why didn't you call the rescue squad?"

Pierce tried to imagine Loren Cappell's reaction to the news that his only child had just been rushed to the hospital after attempting suicide. "Have you ever met her father, Frank?"

"No."

"If you ever do, you'll know the answer to your question."

Francis had then helped in arranging the private ambulance to Global. Waiting for the paramedics, Pierce had sat beside Julia, holding her hand. Her fingers felt cold and he was frightened by the pallor that lingered in her face, although Francis assured him that really, she was fine. He would not be releasing her if she were not. "The people at Global are great, Pierce. Nothing's going to happen to her."

Yet something apparently *was* happening—something Pierce could not fathom—and it was starting to erode his conviction in Diane's parting prophecy. Standing aside so that the medical personnel could load Julia into the ambulance, Pierce had only known that he could not bear it if Diane's words to him—spoken five years ago and once again burning in his ears—turned out to be wrong.

FOUR

Eight years earlier

DIANE DID NOT WALK; SHE FLOATED. Her ability to glide effortlessly through space was the first of her many amazing qualities which captured Pierce's attention. That, and how the warm afternoon September sun shimmered on her golden hair, swept up from her neck in a tousled bun. She looked like a dancer—slender, lithe and willowy. Several other male classmates noticed, too. During a guys-only happy hour Pierce's first year of law school, the conversation had turned to rating the physical merits of the females in their eighty-student section. Diane had placed at the top in several categories.

Yet she remained elusive. She had the uncanny ability to arrive one minute before the professors walked in, and would disappear within seconds after their final word. In a cut-throat environment where it seemed everyone was competing to be noticed, her self-effacing behavior became conspicuous. By deduction, however, he reasoned that Diane had been the one to set the curve on a couple tests—an intimidating combination of beauty and brains who firmly kept her admirers at a distance.

Spring term of their second year, they both were in a class that explored the legal concept of Fraud; no exam, just a project which, true to the course catalogue, required them to design a presentation and instruct their peers on a particular case involving intentionally false misrepresentation. The professor paired Pierce with Diane to analyze a corporate contract for "wrongdoing one in his property rights by dishonest methods or schemes," and "deprivation of something of value by trick, chicane, or overreaching." (*Carpenter* quoting *McNally v. United States*, quoting *Hammerschmidt v. United States* when all was properly cited.) Unlike most women with whom Pierce interacted, Diane did not attempt to flirt when she approached him or become tongue-tied. In fact, her seeming to be oblivious to the fact that they were two incredibly attractive young people caused him to wonder if, like the goddess whose name she bore, she was uninterested in men or perhaps already married. His eyes dropped to double-check her left hand for a ring while, matter-of-factly, a planner in her bare hand, Diane asked, "So, do you want to each do some preliminary research, and then we have a starting point?" When he did not reply immediately, she quickly added, "That's usually a pretty fair and efficient way to handle group work: everybody comes to the table with something."

Pierce had never realized how blue her eyes were until she was looking directly at him, waiting with deliberate patience, which prompted his reply: "Sure."

"I'll stake out a table in the cafeteria. You don't have any classes on Friday, do you?"

"No."

And before he could impress her by answering in more than just a monosyllable for the second time, she handed him a sticky note, on which was written her name and phone number in handwriting that almost seemed like calligraphy. She asked for his number, then jotted it down in her planner on one of the spaces allocated for Friday. "Nine o'clock then. See you round."

Pierce spent hours preparing; at that appointment, he was determined to prove, with his meticulous research and detailed outline, that he deserved her respect, which for some reason, he wanted—badly. He arrived a quarter of an hour early, and his being there first seemed to surprise her when she walked in at exactly 8:58. He smiled once she was seated, and positioned the screen of his Samsung so she could see it. "I just had a few ideas that I thought were worth investigating."

For the next several minutes, Diane listened attentively, on a couple occasions holding her fingers in front of her mouth, as if to remind herself to listen first and ask questions later. She nodded in all the right places and turned to face him as he fleshed out the information on the screen, her forehead puckered attentively. When Pierce finished, she nodded almost imperceptibly several times, and then proceeded to summarize his entire argument succinctly, although she did intersperse her rendition with "um" on a few occasions.

"That's pretty much what I thought we could do," Pierce agreed, proud of his work once his new partner had finished her synopsis of it. "Can I get you anything to drink?"

"I have water, but if *you* need something, go ahead." Briskly, she pulled out her own tablet, but did not turn it on, even after she began. "One of the constant phrases we've heard in this class, is 'Don't focus on what seems obvious.' So with that in mind, I think the basis for prosecution of this case should be *Sherman*, not *Clayton*." And for the next twenty minutes, with all the confidence of moral certainty, she eviscerated virtually everything he had just said. Immersed in the need to prove willful intent to create a *per se* monopoly, Diane's aloofness melted. He was drawn in by the inflection of her words, matched by her hands' graceful but emphatic gestures and her widening eyes. "The relevant sections of all the cases are here," she added as she finished. Her fingers touched a few keys rapidly and she brought the file to the screen. "I want to improve the lay out, of course, highlight some of the key phrases, add a few visual effects. You know—eye candy. Just staring at a screen filled with words is boring."

At Diane's behest, they met twice more to refine their presentation, and the third time to practice. He would open and close; she would explain the substantive arguments. She also insisted they go first "to set the bar, and besides, other than being last, going first leaves the strongest impression, and I want an A."

"Have you ever settled for anything less?"

"Chemistry," was the curt reply, "my junior year of high school." She smiled. "It's why I'm in law school and not med school."

The morning of their presentation, she was twenty-five minutes early, clad in a navy skirt tailored to accentuate her dancer's form. Her hair was smooth instead of tousled, and she was wearing more than mascara. In three-inch pumps, she was slightly taller than he was —a striking figure in a Nordic goddess kind of way. She seemed anxious as she double-checked details, but definitely not nervous. Having prepared so scrupulously so that nothing could go wrong, their entire presentation proceeded smoothly; she had even correctly anticipated Dr. Gray-Dodson's questions, and they could both answer with self-assured poise.

For the remaining class sessions, most of which were dominated by other students' in-comparison-sub-par reports on viable options for dealing with specific cases of fraud, Diane sat beside Pierce in the back row, taking notes punctuated by exclamation points when she agreed and question marks when she did not. Passive she was not. She even turned listening into a contest.

The last time the class met in early May before finals, Pierce had asked her if she wanted to do something fun as soon as exams were over. "I have tickets for the Red Sox on Sunday."

"I'm leaving for D.C. on Saturday. My internship starts on Monday." A statement that veiled the fact she was saying no.

"Well, maybe next fall, once you get back."

"Maybe."

"Is your internship at a private firm? Or at a government agency?"

"Please don't think I'm the type to name drop in order to impress you." And Pierce at that moment almost hated Diane Garret for resuming her original standoffishness. Why couldn't she reveal a detail most of their classmates practically advertised? An internship was definitely not an intensely private matter! But by then, he at least realized why Diane's remote demeanor had for so long irritated him: he was totally, sail-to-the-farthest-shores infatuated with her.

FIVE

Pierce checked social media sites to see if Diane was posting any photos of herself in front of the Lincoln Monument, Supreme Court or any other capital city landmarks; other than her student profile, she was devoid of any online presence. When he searched her name on the internet, it yielded nothing, other than suggestions to spell her first name with two n's or the last name with two t's. True, five other Diane Garrets did pop up, but they lived in the wrong states, were of a different race, or were the wrong ages. However, without Diane's realizing it, some of her replies to Pierce's casual questions, whispered during class, had revealed which courses she had registered for in the fall.

"My dad thinks I should make a few changes to my fall classes, given our company's recently revised business model," Pierce told the registrar when he met with him to request adding and dropping courses. The registrar, aware Pierce's father was one of the university's largest private contributors, had immediately complied and revised Pierce's schedule. Now Pierce too was taking both Mergers and Acquisitions and Structuring Venture Capital, classes where, because there was only one section for each, he would be certain to be with Diane.

On the first day of the term, Pierce hung out in the hall, pretending to be on an important call. He nodded his greeting to Diane as she slipped by moments before class was scheduled to begin, and before she walked through the door, spoke to his imaginary contact. "Hey, I'll get back to you as soon as class is over; it's about to start." Pierce followed Diana in and slid into the seat next to hers. *How was your summer?* He typed in a large font as the lecture started, and angled the screen so she could read it.

She mouthed the word: "Marvelous!" before turning her full focus to the professor's remarks.

He had to move quickly to catch up with Diane before she floated off from their second class together. "Hey! I couldn't help but notice we have two classes together."

"Not really surprising since we *are* both pursuing a degree in Law and Business," she said, not even deigning to look at him over her shoulder.

"So I was thinking maybe we could work together again. Look," Pierce reached out and took her arm so that she was forced to stop and face him. "I learned more in the one class that I took with you than in any other class here. You are an awesome study partner."

Perhaps she thought she could stare him down, but when he refused to avert his eyes, she lowered hers. "I'm not sure if I can fit more time on campus into my schedule."

"I can come to wherever you are." He waited while she stared at the sidewalk. "Do you want me to admit that you are so much smarter than I am? Then I admit it; I'm going to use you—for your mind."

Suddenly, Diane met his gaze and held it, almost to the point where her fixed attention became rude, even disconcerting before she laughed. "Actually," she smiled, "I'm the one who will be using you."

"Fine. When and where should we meet?"

Tuesday mornings, after her class on Capital Market Regulation, became Pierce's favorite time of the week. Several people asked him if they were going out; he let them think so because then he and Diane were left alone in their corner of the cafeteria. Yet even though she materialized each week and even sat with him in their two mutual classes, their partnership was solely devoted to becoming better law students. Because Pierce had two older sisters, he thought he had developed a decent sense of what women were like—until he encountered Diane. She was the least inquisitive female Pierce had ever met. She asked no questions about his family or past, with the exception of an inquiry about his undergraduate major. (When she heard "Economics" her reply was maybe *that* was why he found it so difficult to consider other points of view.) Nor did she inquire about his hobbies and interests. It was clear that she had every intention of remaining enigmatic—although she did answer some of his direct questions about Europe: What had she seen? ("Mainly Scandinavia, but they did spend a week in London.") What did she think of it? ("London had far too much to see in only a week!") What was her favorite experience? ("Walking the streets of Stockholm at midnight while there was still day light.") Only when their conversation honed in on their class work, did the real Diane emerge—animated, vibrant. In her intellectual element, she laughed. If their arms touched or his hand brushed hers, she did not pull away.

In early December, Pierce announced he was taking her to lunch. "My treat, since I am the one who roped you into this deal, and talked you into continuing it for both winter and spring term." They had registered once again for some of the same classes. Before she could answer, he picked up her book bag. "Going to lunch with me is the only way you'll get this back, unless, of course, you make a scene which is not your style. Do you like Chinese? There's a great place just up Massachusetts Avenue."

Diane retreated into her reserved shell; Pierce assumed she was about to say no. Instead, she sighed and assented, as if against her better judgment: "I'll need to leave by 2:00."

Part of the secret to Diane's semblance of floating, Pierce discovered, was her walking incredibly fast. The normal thirty-minute trek was completed in a less than twenty-five. Their verbal exchanges were brief and limited to random observations about various buildings' architecture. They didn't have to wait long for a table, and their sesame chicken (hers) and Kung Pao beef (his) was served quickly. Still, there was a strained silence while they waited. "A conversation is in order, Mr. Pierce."

"So why Law and Business, Miss Garret?" he opened.

She smiled with the assurance that this was a safe question. "It's part of my master plan."

"To make a lot of money as a corporate lawyer? Or to go after the bad guys on Wall Street?"

"Neither. I want to help companies become incredibly profitable and then make them realize they need to enter into mutually beneficial partnerships with their local public schools."

"It sounds like you have that written down somewhere."

"I've written down every goal since I was in high school and heard about a Harvard study where the three percent of people who'd written down their goals earned ten times as much as the other 97% of their class combined."

"So why the desire to make companies the benefactors of education?"

"Corporations are like wealthy people who can be persuaded that first, their image and reputation will be enhanced if they display some *noblesse oblige*. Furthermore, their continued success is only possible if they have easy access to a talented pool of educated workers. In one board meeting, one articulate spokesperson could convince a board of directors to appropriate more money to a district than the district could raise with a levy or bond issue. Individual voters are far more selfish; they claim a few hundred dollars of additional tax will bankrupt them. What they mean is that they don't see how they will personally benefit. School districts with a bunch of older voters especially are at risk of their students receiving an education that won't allow them to compete. Corporate sponsorship would level the playing field, a couple districts at a time." A few questions more and Diane revealed she had researched and written a proposal for her idea as an undergrad.

"Where did you go to college?"

She dismissed his question: "No place that an Ivy Leaguer such as yourself has ever heard of." Nevertheless, she continued to speak of potential ways to change educational funding and even teacher training with the same passion that their coursework evoked. When the alarm on her phone rang (her reminder to leave), her lunch was virtually untouched. Still, she immediately stood up, and Pierce helped her into her coat. Then her hand grazed his back, and her chin glanced his shoulder as she drew toward him. "Sorry for rambling. Thanks for listening." Pierce decided that for Diane, such a gesture could qualify as a hug. He asked the waiter for a box and that evening ate her sesame chicken for his supper, remembering how he loved her company.

SIX

Sometimes, on a particularly cold day, Diane would accept Pierce's offer to buy her coffee. They had gone to lunch together a few more times, too, and could now talk about more than class work. However, her personal life was still closed off to him, and she had gently admonished him not to ask about it: "I think it was one of the Roosevelts who said that small minds talk about people, good minds talk about events, and great minds talk about ideas. Since I'm blonde, far too many people already assume I have a brain the size of a pea, so I refuse to talk about anything that would feed into that perception. Don't *you* want to be more than a pretty face?" (It was the first time she had ever acknowledged that she found him attractive.)

Once they discovered their politics were essentially aligned, critiquing the positions on the "other side" became a safe topic of conversation, too. Plus, they both found bioethical issues interesting and often refined their mutual responses to euthanasia, health care, and cloning when walking to the T so she could connect to the green line. Still, he often wondered if to Diane, Conrad Pierce was simply a cerebral sparring partner.

He also wondered, if Diane were removed from an academic setting, would he finally learn more about her? His opportunity to find out came in early March, when Pierce's mother called him to say his grandfather (her dad) and his namesake was turning 90. The occasion would be celebrated the last Saturday in April. "He can't hear any more, the dear, and I think a lot of people will only confuse him. Quite frankly, at 90, there aren't many of his friends to invite anyway so it will just be our family." His sisters, their husbands and children would of course be there. "I know the timing isn't ideal, right before finals, but your grandfather doesn't turn 90 every day either."

"I'll be there," Pierce promised,

He waited until early April to ask Diane to accompany him. "I have a great idea about how we could study right before exams—no interruptions, just a good chunk of time devoted to the review of everything we've learned about Taxation of Corporate Mergers and Advanced Mediation."

"So do we stay in the cafeteria all night? Or hijack the dining room in Dao Garden?"

"I can arrange for us to spend six hours driving to Connecticut and back."

"Why do we need to drive to Connecticut in order to study?"

"Because my grandfather is turning 90, and I think you'd enjoy meeting him and the rest of my family."

Diane flipped open her planner. Pierce knew it was a test. If she refused, he would understand he was merely a wall against which she could bounce her ideas. If she accepted, he could assume that his ardor for her might one day be reciprocated. Diane closed her planner. "I need to check on something first. But I will try. I want to ace Taxation."

In one of the rare text messages she sent him, she confirmed the next day that she could indeed go. They decided to leave on Friday at 1:00. He rented a car, since he'd found that maintaining his own vehicle in Cambridge was burdensome; besides, there was no need for one on campus. He volunteered to pick her up.

"Not necessary. I'll just have an overnight bag. You can take most of my books home with you and bring them along."

Because Diane was hardcore, and because the Massachusetts Turnpike to I-84 was an easy drive, for over two hours they really did study. However, when Diane saw the signs for New Haven, she closed her notes and asked why he had not chosen to attend Yale. "Because my father went to Harvard and would have disowned me if I had even applied."

"You need to fill me in on your family so I don't look like an idiot."

"Well, the birthday boy is Grandpa. He went into the Army Air Corp right after Pearl Harbor. He's hard of hearing now, but if you can make him understand that you want to hear about what he did during the War, he'll do most of the talking. Ever since he went on an Honor Flight, he's been willing to share stories I've never heard, and they're really pretty interesting."

"Grandma?"

"Died when I was in high school."

"And your father?"

"Grandpa bought a store where people could buy milk and pump gas when he got back from Europe in1946. He spun off some franchises. Dad helps him run the business. His friends call him Hank."

"I prefer to call him Mr. Pierce. Your mother?"

"Celia—I suppose Mrs. Pierce to you—is devoted to the arts and does a lot of volunteer work."

"You said you have sisters?"

"Catherine is ten years older and married to Steve. He's a surgeon, and they have two kids: Jordan, who, if he isn't playing soccer, is playing some soccer video game, and Josie.

"How old is she?"

"I think going on ten? I know Catherine skipped my high school graduation because Josie had just been born. My other sister, Candace, is also a stay-at-home mom, and her daughter Brianna is three."

"Candace's husband is . . . ?"

"Brad."

Diane closed her eyes and counted off one finger for each name: "Catherine, Steve, Jordan and Josie. Candace and Brad have Brianna. Talk arts with mom, World War Two with grandpa and franchises with dad. Got it."

Pierce would later recall how quiet Diane had become, looking out the window at the homes along tree-lined Nearwater Lane and then the expanse of Holly Pond, visible from the road as they drove across Noroton Neck. They pulled into the circular driveway of his parents' home. "Did you grow up here?" she asked, scanning the lawn, the house.

"My parents moved here the year I was born."

"I would have loved playing in whatever that is that looks like a castle tower."

"I pretended it was a lighthouse when I played Revolution." He pointed. "See the windows at the top? That's where I could signal to the American colonists that the Redcoats were coming."

"What a total history geek."

"Guilty as charged. I'll get your door."

She was pushing the visor's mirror back up when he reached the passenger side. She had applied lip gloss and smoothed her hair. He held the back of her arm as they climbed the flight of steps to the front door, her eyes taking in the soaring windows, the balcony. Maria, the housekeeper, opened the door and directed them back to the pool, where his mother was meeting with caterers to put last minute touches on her instructions for the party.

Celia Pierce embodied the stereotype of the wealthy suburban wife who played tennis five days a week and was perpetually tan from boating all summer. Her dark hair was expertly styled, and her nails had been painted red that morning. Espadrilles, Capri pants, a silk sweater. She greeted Diane graciously and thanked her for coming.

The moment of truth; Pierce waited to see whether the vivacious or diffident Diane would emerge. "I wouldn't miss it." Diane's voice was effervescent. "How often does one receive an invitation to a ninetieth birthday party? I absolutely love your view of the water!" By the end of their initial conversation, his mother and Diane were headed to the gallery to inspect Celia's collection of impressionist paintings. "Now how exactly do you frame them to prevent light damage?" Diane was asking.

Catherine and Steve's arrival occurred while Pierce and Diane were at the dock and was made known when they noticed Jordan's juggling a soccer ball in the backyard. "Something tells me you're a mid-fielder," Diane commented as Jordan shook hands a little awkwardly with his uncle's girlfriend. She followed up with questions that elicited his nephew's soccer resume, and then asked, "Who do you think is going to win the World Cup this year?" When Jordan replied he was rooting for the Netherlands, Diane and Jordan entered into a brief but expert conversation about some of the Dutch players, while Pierce could only listen in astonishment as Diane explained, "I only follow Bayern-Munich, so I know van Bommel and Roben, but van Persie is supposed to be *really* fun to watch." Jordan was charmed.

So was Josie, who was swimming in the pool, which had just been opened yesterday. Diane spent almost a half hour on the deck, throwing diving sticks for Josie to retrieve until the little girl finally decided the water was still too cold. "I told her it would be freezing!" Catherine sighed with maternal superiority, and found Diane a willing listener to her rant about stubborn, willful pre-adolescents. Diane was equally attentive to Candace's lament about the vicissitudes of potty-training. Brianna, though, was most taken in by Diane, who turned out to be an authority on all the Disney princesses and had no problem understanding three-year-old-speech or making cupcakes out of Lego Duplos.

Had they talked about family prior to this trip, Pierce would not have put it past Diane to research each of his relatives' interests, but her latent proficiency on such a variety of topics surprised him. He tried to envision her watching soccer, and wondered if she had a lot of younger siblings. (That would explain her rapport with kids.) Her only deficit area appeared to be boating, a shortcoming his father was quick to remedy by taking her out, along with Steve and Brad, on his new Sealine F530 the next morning.

The highlight of the weekend, though, was the birthday party, painstakingly planned and Celia-lavish. Other than semi-deafness, Pierce's grandfather was doing amazingly well for a nonagenarian. He had played nine holes of golf on Thursday, his actual birthday, and was still swimming five days a week to help the arthritis in his knees. He was delighted to meet Diane. "You look just like Catherine Deneuve." A surreptitious internet search allowed Pierce to conclude that his grandfather's comparison was appropriate, and Diane did exude a sort of French film star quality in a black jersey sheath that emphasized her slim silhouette. (His eavesdropping on Celia, Catherine and Candace affirmed they approved of her outfit, too.) She asked Grandpa about his war experience, appeared to be rapt by his account of a bomb run over Bremen, and danced with him to his favorite Tommy Dorsey songs that were playing much louder than usual over the home audio system.

On Sunday, Celia insisted on a family brunch, served in the dining room, which like every other room in the house featured fabulous water views. She tried to convince Pierce and Diane to stay for the afternoon, but Pierce was adamant that they leave by noon. "Diane will make sure that we study all the way back to Cambridge." The round of good-byes and wishes for a safe journey began. Hugs and kisses from Brianna and his sisters. "Lovely to meet you and do come again" from his parents. Pierce and Diane drove in silence, even after they were on the freeway. At the second bridge, Diane commented on how taken she was with the water.

"This summer, then, we should go to Grandpa's place on Martha's Vineyard. Candace and Catherine both spend a lot of time there, and after this weekend, I would assume they and the kids would welcome you with open arms. You made a good impression." He tentatively reached for her hand, and when Diane did not stiffen or draw it away, Pierce brought it to his lips to kiss and then held her palm and fingers against his thigh as he drove with his left hand, again in silence. They were almost to Bridgeport before she reminded him that they needed to study again, and reached into the back seat for her annotated copies of all the articles they had read for Advanced Mediation. (She despised reading on a screen.) They reviewed all the way to Cambridge.

Once again, Pierce offered to take her home, and once again she refused. "If I didn't know better, I would think you were hiding something."

"No need to go out of your way."

After he dropped the car off, she relented to an early supper, so they walked to a deli, picked up some sandwiches and then passed the Kennedy School to sit along the Charles River. That was where Pierce kissed—really kissed—Diane for the first time and where she kissed him back. Where she sat with her head against his shoulder, watching the joggers and walkers take advantage of the warm spring weekend, until she stood because it was time to go if she wanted to make her train connection, and she still needed to put the finishing touches on one of her two take home exams. They walked up Dunster Street to the station, holding hands, and he insisted on going down the escalators with her and waiting in the subterranean vault as a street musician played folk music of his invention in front of his open guitar case, his voice echoing off the cracked tile.

Pierce did not want Diane to leave him; he wanted to rewind the whole weekend, to see her hair blowing in the breeze as she stood on the dock; to watch her enter the room, stunning in black, and catch Steve's approving wink; to look over at her, with Brianna in her lap at brunch, counting each blueberry before they ate it. The train's rumble drew them closer to the tracks. "Will you be able to carry everything?"

"I've made it before from the airport with two full-size suitcases."

When the headlight from the train beamed into view, Pierce enveloped Diane in a genuine, pressed-against-her embrace. "I had a wonderful time," she whispered in his ear, her thumb caressing the back of neck. "You have a delightful family." He waited until the door of the subway car folded shut and waved to her once she had sat down and looked out the window. As soon as Pierce re-emerged into the street, he pulled out his phone and sent her a text: *Miss you already.*

SEVEN

BECAUSE DIANE WAS THE ULTIMATE STUDENT, their relationship returned, that first week of May, to its pre-Connecticut routine. Even though their last final was the same, they had been divided alphabetically into separate rooms. "How did it go?" Pierce asked as soon as they rendezvoused by the arches of Wasserstein.

"Very solid," was her assessment.

"Then, since our law school career has come to an auspicious close, I suggest a celebration: the Eastern Standard, Kenmore Square. I reserved a table for 8:30."

One of the first questions his father had asked Diane had concerned her future plans. She had responded with a laugh, and as usual, skillfully deflected the query into her personal affairs: "Right now, it's to do well on finals." With finals over, Pierce wanted to ask the same question himself. He suspected she probably had been sending out resumes for weeks without telling him. For all he knew, she already had secured a six-figure job. But if she hadn't, his family had connections, and now that she had met them, she could benefit from his dad making a few calls.

"Do we have time for a walk?" Diane asked.

"It all depends on how long we walk."

"It won't be long." And they were off at her effortless speed, heading toward the bank of the Charles River.

In a relationship that had been marked by enigma, the silence as they walked was nothing new. "Something you want to say?" Pierce finally ventured.

"On Sunday, you said, you wondered if I was hiding something," Diane began.

"I see." He wanted to keep the mood light. "A moment of confession."

"It is." Her voice caught on her words, and he followed as she veered off the path and walked across the grass until they were somewhat by themselves. She stood facing the water with her arms crossed. From the way she was clenching her jaw, he thought she was going to cry, but she remained dry-eyed and silent. Waiting, Pierce assumed the same stance, mindlessly watching a trio of runners. Once aware that they were no longer visible, he gently prodded her shoulder with his own.

Diane took a deep breath, and spoke so softly, Pierce had to concentrate on just hearing her words. "I knew you had money," he could hear her say, "from the moment I first saw you on the steps of Langdell Hall. You walk it, you talk it, but for me, so does virtually every other person here. But when we turned into the drive of your parents' house with its pool and private dock, four garages, and what? Six? Seven bedrooms? If I've learned one thing since I've moved out East, it's that real estate prices here are obscene. So, when I finished up my essays on Sunday, I did a little research. The Fairfield County Auditor's office lists the value of your family's home at $6.2 million."

"And this is relevant because?"

"Because research is a chain, and one link leads to another. It didn't take long to find out that I had danced with a billionaire. Apparently, your grandfather, Conrad, has a rather well-known last name in the financial world. That little 'store where people could buy milk and pump gas' has more than 'some' franchises." Her voice began to quote: "'674 locations in seven states, although only 527 dispense gasoline. He also diversified in the late 1970s and invested in utilities and insurance. *Forbes* now estimates his personal fortune at $1.25 billion.'"

Growing up, Pierce had often heard Grandpa Conrad chuckle as he remarked he had done pretty well for a Pollack whose first job was in a rope factory. Since the chain of gas and convenience stores—which Pierce and his siblings had always called "Grandpa Con's"—was ubiquitous in New England and New York, he had always had a sense of his family's retail empire. But he and his sisters had always been expected to work at them forty hours each week in the summer (although he had been able to schedule his shifts around his baseball tournaments). What money they earned, they were expected to invest or give to a charity of their choice. When they were in college, they had performed clerical work in one of the many offices that were also part of Grandpa Con's network. Grandpa, and to some extent, his parents believed in "working your way up." Catherine, Candace and he had also been instructed to never advertise their family's wealth. They were raised to *not* be elitist snobs, and had always been focused on working hard, not flaunting money. Pierce failed to see why his grandfather's fortune was an issue for Diane.

"So how does this tie in with your hiding something?"

"Because your parents' monthly mortgage payments are probably more than my mother makes in an entire year! I'm not used to dealing with an income bracket that includes not even a couple hundred people nationwide."

Pierce watched as her fingernails dug into the flesh of her folded arms. She tilted her head back, and a single tear leaked from the corner of her eye. He was suddenly worried. Maybe he didn't see a problem, but Diane certainly did, and she was going to act on her perceptions, not his. He wrapped his arms around her waist. She did not relax against him; she even stiffened. "Hey, study partner. You understand something I don't. Explain it to me."

"Okay. It's time for the life history of Diane Garret, which is not pretty and doesn't take long to tell." She recounted the details matter-of-factly, looking over his shoulder, a summary of essential information, and only with the grudging indulgence of the court. "First, Garret is not my real name. I chose it because I always loved Cinderella, and how she started out, locked in the *garret* by her cruel step-mother until a glass slipper later, she becomes the kingdom's princess. My real name was Gunderson. My father walked out on Mom when I was two, and my sister Debbie and I were raised in a trailer park in Toledo, Ohio. Mom was a waitress and worked her way up to bartender. Debbie dropped out of high school her senior year after my nephew Troy was born. I was in eighth grade, but I knew that if all there was in life was a trailer, a sub-minimum wage job, and a man who would leave me alone with a kid, I should just kill myself right then."

The thought flashed through Pierce's mind that Diane was like one of those embedded CIA agents who adopts a new identity, but rather than inventing a past for herself, she had simply buried it. She avoided all the situations where small talk was an expectation or found ways to let others speak while she listened, unless, of course, she could engage them to discuss ideas. Her cool detachment suddenly made sense. He held her closer, and she understood it was his way of assuring her she could continue, even though her every muscle remained taut.

"My summer assignment for ninth grade Honors English was to write a personal narrative, and for some reason I chose to write about that moment. The teacher, Mrs. Printz, wrote me a really lovely note, told me how impressed she was with my writing. I *knew* I was smart. (Mom always said Dad's problem was that he was a genius.) But Mrs. Printz was the one who convinced me to keep my GPA high. She watched out for me throughout high school, helped me realize that I could find a way to afford college. She found out I was pretty good at soccer and suggested that might help me win a scholarship. So between the grades and soccer, this sort of prestigious division three school—they have a reputation as a "catalytic college"—gave me a lot of money—even though they couldn't call it an athletic scholarship. I helped run summer soccer camps for spending money. I aced the LSAT and was valedictorian, so Harvard Law came to me. My college coach's sister-in-law lives in Brookline and is a lawyer herself, and agreed to give me room and board if I nannied for her two kids. That's why I've always needed to leave campus every day by 2:00—so I can pick them up at school by 3:30."

"And also why you've never let me take you home." He kissed her forehead. "When did you change your name?"

"Right before I came to law school." (That explained why his efforts to uncover information about her had fallen short.) "My goal was to acquire the Harvard degree, return to the Midwest where an Ivy League diploma really impresses people, become a corporate lawyer and eventually champion corporate funding for public schools. The last thing in the world I wanted was to get romantically involved with anyone—here, now, ever."

He kissed her again. "Our being together doesn't mean you have to sacrifice your goals. Not that I want you to return to the Midwest, but we have corporations and public schools that need help here."

"I've read my Jane Austen enough to know that my upbringing is not going to exactly recommend me for *entre* to your world."

"My world?"

"Yes! Your world—where no one has ever lived on fish sticks or had a mother who slept with a mechanic so he'd change the oil in her rusted-out van for free. You never pawned your mother's wedding ring that she never wore anyway so you could buy soccer cleats to try out for the high school team."

"That doesn't have to be your world anymore."

For the first time since they had been standing by the water, Diane looked at him directly, her palms against his chest. "I can leave the world, and I used this past weekend as an opportunity to prove to myself I'm not intimidated by wealth. But I can't leave the people. I've denied my father and refused to use his name, but I still want—and need—to take care of my mom and Debbie and give Troy real options."

"And you should and you will."

Her signature withering eye-contact, and then: "With money that *I* have earned."

"You can send them every penny you ever make."

"Then how do I live?"

"Well, remember I sort of *do* have a job in the family business. I think I can safely say that I'll make enough to support us both."

Not at all how he had wanted to suggest marriage. Since the kiss beside the river on Sunday, he had been flirting with the idea that this summer, he would take her to Martha's Vineyard. Grandpa Con had always told him that he wanted Pierce to use the diamond he had given Grandma on their fiftieth wedding anniversary for an engagement ring someday. The ring, the beach at sunset . . . Yet, there was no time for that, because Diane was asking, "Is that a proposal?"

"Yes—and not at all how it was supposed to be." Still, he dropped to one knee, hoping she would be amused and yet convinced that the moment was authentic. "Diane Garret, will you marry me?"

"No." The swiftness of her refusal stunned him. Pierce could hardly force himself to listen as she stated that as soon as she had discovered his pedigree, she had vowed to end their liaison—and had waited until after finals so that he would not be distracted. She apologized; she never intended to hurt him; in a moment of weakness, she had miscalculated and mistakenly, as it turned out, allowed herself to accept Pierce's invitation to the ball. A lucky find on some outfits at her favorite re-sale store dispensed with the need for a fairy godmother. Once she was a guest in his parents' home, her only concern had been not to embarrass herself, or Pierce. But Diane Garret, unlike her inspiration, Cinderella, could see only the pitfalls of proving that her foot fit his glass slipper. Happily-ever-after was not a possibility.

As always, Diane was in control as she explained: "I am not going to spend the rest of my life hiding my story. I have for these last three years, and it's been *exhausting*. And I'm not going to broadcast a rags-to-riches tale either, so that people will always question whether I married you for your family's money." For a brief moment, her detachment lapsed, and Diane lifted his face gently in hands. "I *do* love you . . . I've had to admit that to myself. And I love you far too much to simply turn you into my Prince Charming. I hate myself for hurting you, but I am certain that someday, a fabulous young woman from your own *milieu* will make you very happy, and everyone will know she loves you for yourself alone. That is what you *deserve*." She bent down and kissed his cheek.

Pierce willed himself to watch her walk away—only because he knew that he would never see her again. Of that, he was certain, and he wanted to remember forever how she truly did float. Without looking back, Diane Garret drifted beyond his reach, out of his life, leaving him still beguiled, but now spited and spurned.

EIGHT

Pierce stayed up most of the first night in what he would later consider his life A.D. (After Diane.) Huddled up on the couch, he had spent hours on the internet reading every mention of the name *Diane Gunderson*, from team rosters, to articles about her soccer prowess, to pieces she had written for high school and college publications. Conference MVP and named to Ohio's first team. An opinion piece on the Presidential election. A perfect score on the LSAT. A black and white photograph that made him recall Grandpa Con's comment about Catherine Deneuve.

Pierce's father telephoned the next day. He asked about exams, reminded Pierce to call his mom, who wanted to make plans to celebrate his graduation—all preliminaries that allowed Hank to segue into the real reason for the call. "I made some inquiries about your friend Miss Garret."

Hank refused to use expletives and had forbidden their utterance in his presence, so Pierce bit his tongue. Still, it was difficult to not end the conversation right then, but it was inevitable; besides, he would have to deal with it sooner or later. "And what did you find, Dad? That Diane's hard to track down? Try Gunderson. That was her name until about three and a half years ago."

"My people found that out already, Son."

"So what else did they discover?"

"Enough to make me think that a pre-nuptial agreement is in order, if, of course, that is the direction in which you are headed. And I assume, since this is the first girl you've brought home since you've been of marriageable age, my surmise is warranted. Now, rather impressively, Diane has no debt—"

"But she *was* raised in a mobile home and has some rather, shall we say, unsavory relatives. Anything else that would make you think she's a gold digger?"

"Pierce, I never said that. She is a *beautiful* girl. Your mother and sisters—everybody really—was so impressed by her looks, her taste, her manners—"

"You forgot intelligence," Pierce interrupted again. "Did you check out the article from her college paper about her being inducted into *Phi Beta Kappa*? If you search on the internet, that article pops up on the second page, toward the bottom and—"

This time it was his father who cut in. "Look, Pierce, I can tell from your tone that I've upset you, which is that last thing I want to do. Your mother and I would simply like to get to know Diane better, and we hope she'll join us for whatever we end up doing when we come over to Cambridge for your graduation. I am merely concerned—"

"Not nearly as much as Diane is. Look, Dad—" (The wound from her rejection was still too raw for him to risk talking much longer.) "Diane truly had no idea about the money until she did her own digging after last weekend. She's ended everything."

"Clearly, that's quite unnecessary."

"It is what it is, Dad. I don't really want to talk about it." He hung up and let his dad's follow up call thirty seconds later go to voicemail.

Other than her daily *Good-morning-love-you* texts, Pierce's mom waited a few days before contacting him. Her voice was solicitous as she asked him how he was doing. She knew about Diane. "Your graduation, Pierce. Everyone wants to be there. Are you up for that?"

The image of Diane reading to Brianna rose to mind. "Not really, Mom."

"What about Grandpa? He's always been so proud of all that you kids have done when it comes to education."

"Mom?" Pierce sought for a way to ask. "Does he know?"

"I'll explain it to him, Dear. I promise, it won't be awkward for you."

The photographs taken on Pierce's graduation day all showed him smiling, even though he felt guilty when he saw the words *in absentia* behind Diane's name in the program. His receiving a law degree? To be expected, a legacy at Harvard, his decision to pursue law an obvious choice for someone who would one day be responsible for running a profitable conglomerate. For Diane, a doctorate of jurisprudence was a true accomplishment, and she had absented herself from it to ensure that their parting was final. But Pierce continued to smile out of habit, even when someone asked, "Is it true that Diane's already working for that corporation—what's its name—in Cincinnati?"

He moved to mid-town Manhattan to learn more about what was still the newest part of Grandpa Con's holdings, insurance. He worked out every morning but Sunday, and was even in better shape than when he was playing ball. He arrived in the office by 8:00 and was still there at 8:00 every night. He spent Sundays with Grandpa, who had become very determined to impart all the practical lessons he had learned over 70 plus years in business. Pierce allowed himself no time in which to think, even though, as he walked along a crowded street or stepped off an elevator, an occasional sighting of a tall, blonde woman with upswept hair and a graceful figure would unnerve him.

A few weeks after he played golf with Grandpa on his ninety-first birthday, Pierce woke up to the end of his first year without Diane, knowing only that the adage was wrong: time had not healed his wound. Her memory still tormented him.

NINE

In mid-August, Grandpa Con died in his sleep. Because his passing was so sudden, it was a tremendous shock, and Pierce—really the entire family—had operated on automatic pilot for the next few days: the funeral (where Pierce gave the eulogy), the front-page story in *The Times* of Grandpa's accomplishments. Pierce wondered if, even in Cincinnati, Diane had heard the news. He slipped into a daydream where she called to express her condolences, where one thing led to another—a vain fantasy born of his sorrow.

When the week that had passed in a haze was over, the realization that Grandpa would not be there to visit on Sunday started to sink in, and suddenly, Pierce was overwhelmed with the desire to go to Grandpa's place on Martha's Vineyard. He left at 3:00 A.M. Friday morning and was able to drive 80 miles per hour much of the way in his new Jag convertible. ("Consider it a belated graduation gift—and my way of saying 'I'm proud of you for working so hard,'" Grandpa Con had said when they had gone to the dealership to pick it up just last month.)

The weather was idyllic; Gina, a local woman who, along with her husband, maintained Grandpa Con's place, spotted him on the back deck and insisted on cooking him breakfast. "I am so sorry about Mr. Conrad. He was a gentleman who always treated me very good." She also volunteered to go to the store and stock the refrigerator, but he told her that was not necessary. He would only be there through Sunday and would eat out; in fact, she could take the day off. Really, Pierce wanted to be alone. Once she was gone, Pierce grabbed an autobiography of Lincoln (one of Grandpa's favorite people) and a bottle of wine, and strolled down to his private slice of beach to read, to contemplate, to toast Grandpa for a life well-lived. He wore his swim trunks and took some towels, too, knowing that standing in the waves, hypnotized by their rhythm, would soothe the pain left by Grandpa Con's death, as well as the chronic hurt over Diane that was now a constant of his existence.

By late afternoon, lying on his towel after his second foray into the surf and a third glass of cabernet, the words on the page stopped taking intelligible form, and a week of sleep deprivation caught up with him. When Pierce woke, the tide had crept nearly to his towel, although it was not the water's proximity that awakened him. It was a gently insistent female voice: "Excuse me. Excuse me. You might want to move your book."

For a split second, in the shadow, he thought it was Diane—the same ballet-build and cameo coiffure. But this woman was shorter, much darker with tanned olive skin. When she took off her sun glasses, her eyes were brown, the expertly waxed brows black. Pierce sat up languidly, and shifted *A Team of Rivals* away from danger.

"I nearly moved it for you, but if you woke up and realized the book was in a different place, that would be kind of creepy. Besides, you look a little burnt. You probably should get out of the sun."

Years of Celia's etiquette reminders took hold and pushed Pierce up to a standing position so that he could extend his hand. "Thanks for saving the book from irreparable damage. Pierce."

"Julia." A perfunctory shake. "I hope you don't mind. I know this is a private beach, but we have the place next to yours and the ladies that are sometimes here gave me permission to go along the shore. It makes for a better walk." She brushed some strands of hair that were blowing in the stiff breeze away from her mouth and continued to stand there. He had noticed other females over the years eyeing him in the same approving manner, although this one seemed so much younger.

Suddenly self-conscious, he picked up the towel he had been using as pillow and wrapped it around his waist before continuing the conversation. "So your family bought the place next door? I knew it was up for sale last year, but haven't been down since."

"I've actually been here quite a bit this summer, although this week will probably be my last since I really need to start getting ready for college."

"Where will you be going?"

"Harvard."

"That's where I went. Adams House. *'Alteri Seculo.'*" Immediately, the camaraderie of alumni kicked in.

"Was it hard?"

"Just keep up with the reading and go to class. You'll be fine." He sat back down and motioned her to join him. "You already have taken care of the hardest part: getting in."

Julia turned her face and studied the horizon. "I've always wondered if I really got in, or if Daddy made one of his 'calls.'" She looked at him, abashed and lowered her voice confidentially. "I mean, I only got a 1440 on the SAT, and I had friends who scored higher, and *they* didn't get in."

"SATs aren't everything. What about grades?"

"Everybody who applies to Harvard has a minimum of a four point."

"What about travel? Talents?"

"I've gone to Dubai and Hong Kong with Daddy a few times on business, and as for talent, I once auditioned to dance the Plum Fairy."

"As in the Nutcracker Ballet?"

"You know it then? I was in the corps with the New York City Ballet one season."

"I probably saw you. My mother insists we go every year."

"I really scaled back my dancing once I was in high school; it's just a workout now. But I miss the performing, the dresses, the flowers. Daddy said it wouldn't really help me in the long run, though."

"My parents said the same thing about baseball, although they never suggested I should quit or just play for fun. But when I blew out my elbow, their attitude was: 'In the long run, there's so much more you can do in life than throw a curve ball.'"

"I have to confess, I know nothing about baseball. I have no idea what a curveball even is."

"Well, I have no idea how to dance."

"Of course you do. Well, maybe not on point, but everybody can move to music. Here—" impulsively she rocked up on her heels and pulled him up by the hand. "I bet your mother made you take ballroom dancing, didn't she?" He grinned sheepishly. Celia had insisted he take lessons before Catherine's wedding. Julia placed her fingers lightly on his left should and stretched out his right arm. "I follow your lead."

"There's no music."

"Listen to the waves. *One*, two, three. *One*, two, three. A fast waltz."

He shuffled in the sand, and aware of her expectant smile, laughed. "I remember this is what I hated most about dance class. Feeling like I was supposed to talk when it was all I could do to keep time."

"You're doing great." A few more shuffles, and he had managed to move from the towel onto the wetness of the sand. "I noticed the scars on your elbow. You had surgery, didn't you?"

"Yeah, the summer before I was to start college, actually."

"Does Harvard even have a baseball team?"

"It does, but originally, I was supposed to go to Duke and play ball there. When Dad realized that my career was over, he made one of those calls himself, and I ended up in Cambridge, a late admit, with just a 1430 SAT."

"But you probably aced the math portion."

How had she known? They waltzed along the beach, skirting the water, for a few more minutes, and when they stopped, Pierce commented that it was a good thing the beach was secluded so that no one could see them. "It's why our families bought these places, isn't it? To be secluded?" she replied.

"It sounds like you don't like seclusion. Just wait until you've lived at college for a year."

"Maybe. I've just been by myself a lot this summer, and Angelica couldn't come down this weekend."

"If you're by yourself, do you want to stay for supper? I haven't eaten since breakfast, and it was an early one at that."

"Daddy doesn't really like for me to go out when I'm down here."

"We'll order something in, and you can tell me about this Daddy."

"Only if you tell me about yours."

Over crab cakes and bouillabaisse, he discovered Julia's last name was Cappell, and immediately recognized that "Daddy" was the New York real-estate mogul who, coincidentally, owned the office building where he worked, plus an international hotel chain. (Hence the trips to Dubai and Hong Kong.) Currently, he was in Washington D.C. as New York's junior Senator.

She had read in *The Times* (because Daddy insisted she read the paper to keep up with current events) about his grandpa. She was sympathetic, and listened to Pierce's account of Grandpa Con's life. "If you're named for him, and if he was so wonderful, why don't you go by Conrad?"

"In junior high, some of the guys called me Connie, which I absolutely hated because it seemed so girly. By that time, I was pretty hard-core about baseball, and the coach and everyone on the team always called me Pierce. I liked that better."

It had grown dark while they talked, and when she realized it was almost ten, Julia stood up quickly. "I really do need to go. I hate to take my phone with me when I'm at the beach, and I know Daddy has probably tried to call me."

"I'll walk you home."

"Really, no. Just walk me to our beach and watch to make sure I get in."

"Call me to let me know you got in, okay?"

"What's your number?"

He spied an ink pen on the table, and wrote ten digits on her arm. "Can you read it?"

Pierce opened one of the French doors to the deck. The sand forced them to trudge so the walk to beach was languorous, and she commented on the moon reflecting on the water before thanking him for a fun evening. Her dark shape seemed to move faster once she was alone. He heard a door open, and a light from inside transformed some of the back windows into radiant rectangles. His phone rang. "Hello?"

"I'm in. Call if you ever want a dance partner. Daddy's left three messages, so I need to call him back now."

After the exchange of good-byes, Pierce decided to save her number to his contacts. He found it too rich to be a mere coincidence that his last conversation with Grandpa had been about women: "My heart break came in England. She thought her husband had died on D-day, and all of sudden, he came home so she and I were through. But I will tell you this: when I met your grandma, I knew she was a keeper. And someday, you'll find the right one, and you'll know, too. And when that happens, you put that ring I've told you about on her finger and never let her go."

Julia Cappell was indeed a young woman from his own *milieu* and there were indications she might be fabulous. Suddenly, Pierce wanted to give

Diane the chance to prove to him one last time that she was always right. He was too jaded to believe any more, in love at first sight, but he was willing to believe that fate had orchestrated his meeting Julia Cappell and that, more importantly, she could very well be part of his destiny.

TEN

Ten months later

LOREN CAPPELL SAT AT HIS CUSTOMARY table at New York City's Metropolitan Club. He glanced at his Rolex (since cell phones were still strictly prohibited). He'd arrived 15 minutes early just to see how punctual young Pierce would be. It was five minutes 'til 7:00 when Pierce walked in.

One thing for sure: Pierce looked nothing like his dad. He had his mother's Eastern European good looks. Rumor was that he had once had a shot at the Major Leagues, and judging from the width of his shoulders beneath his Italian suit jacket, it was probably true. Cappell stood as Pierce approached and they gripped hands. Cappell always tried to make men wince when they greeted each other the first time—the alpha male instinct. Pierce did not flinch and his own grip was impressively firm. Cappell liked that.

"What will you have to drink, young man?"

"Whatever you are having, Sir."

Smooth. Knows how to avoid doing something that would make him feel like a fool. Catching the waiter's attention, Cappell signaled for another club soda to be brought to the table. Pierce waited a fraction of a second so that the older man sat down first.

"I knew you'd joined here after your grandfather died. Con was a good man. How long has it been, now since he passed?"

"A little under a year."

"I've heard you've been hand-picked to take over."

"I've pretty much been running the insurance side now. My father still oversees the retail part of the business, and my brother-in-law is in charge of the utilities."

"True family operation. That's great. I have no time or patience for shareholders." The waiter served Pierce, and Cappell waited until they were alone before asking, "So, why did you call me up? I know that's pretty direct, but I already have a reputation for being rude, and I hate useless chit chat."

"Do you find Washington frustrating then, Senator?"

"There are days, young man," Cappell leaned forward to share a confidence, "when I curse my decision to run for Congress. All that I'll-change-the-way-Washington-works garbage I spewed during the campaign. My goal now is to not let Washington change me, or I'll come back here and sit with both thumbs up my ass while I watch my money go down the drain." Pierce smiled in response and swizzled the liquid in the glass that had just been set before him. "You want to rent more space? Are you doing such a bang-up job with the insurance division that you need more offices?"

Pierce put his elbows on the table and leaned his chin on his fists, which he had wedged together at the knuckles. "I suspect you already know why I'm here. My business tonight is a completely personal matter."

Cappell's daughter had admitted to him last summer that she had spent one evening with Pierce. Cappells' personal assistant, who monitored Julia's cell phone bill and checked into any unknown numbers as a precaution, had alerted him when his daughter received a text from Pierce during Reading Week in January and at the end of second term as well.

"You wouldn't happen to be referring to my daughter?"

"I know you keep close tabs on her, Senator."

"She's my child, and this world is full of dangerous people."

"I'm here to assure you that I am not one of them."

Cappell leaned back in his chair. This was no boy in front of him. "How old are you, Pierce?"

"I turned thirty in April. I worked for Grandpa for about three years after I finished my undergrad, until we figured out a law degree would be most helpful to the company."

"You know that Julia won't even turn nineteen until July 31st."

"I have considered the fact that Julia was kindergarten when I got my driver's license, yes, Sir. But I also know that difference in age matters less the older one becomes."

Cappell narrowed his eyes. In his own suave way, this man whom he had dismissed as Con's grandson was as direct and to the point as Cappell himself. He wagged his pointer finger at Pierce. "Are you, by chance, asking my permission to marry my daughter?"

"Not exactly. I've spent four hours with her and sent her two text messages wishing her luck on her finals. I trust you understand why I am unwilling to request permission to *marry*. But I would like your permission to become better acquainted. Supervised visits if you wish. My sisters spend a great deal of time at Martha's Vineyard in the summer, and I'm sure they wouldn't mind watching their little brother again."

"In other words, when it's time for Julia to think about a wedding, you want to have cornered the groom market."

"To use a business analogy, yes. But to make sure such a merger would be in both parties' best interest, I need to find out if we are compatible and if we can grow to love each other."

Cappell rubbed the skin between his nose and top lip with the side of his finger and studied the young man in front of him. He liked the fact that Pierce did not turn away from his scrutiny.

"Listen here. You are not to take her to any public place where reporters could see her. I hate reporters. I don't want them twisting her actions. Next, keep her out of social media. Finally, if you decide you are—what was the word? 'Compatible?'—you are not to mention love, let alone marriage, until after she graduates from college."

"Those are reasonable requests. I'll be sure honor them. Anything else?"

"Yeah. You do anything to her that you would not do in front me, Pierce, and I'll find out and see that you are whipped, tormented and deprived of your food."

"I understand, sir."

Cappell noticed his signature threat had rolled off Pierce, who, from the way the corners of his mouth twitched, seemed amused. Such a sense of humor could be important in a marriage; its absence in his own made him appreciate humor's value. Loren hoped Julia had sense enough to see that getting to know Pierce would be worth her while. *But would Conrad Pierce grow tired of waiting?*

Loren winked at Pierce. "Now, what do you want to eat? My treat. I hear the prime rib tonight is particularly excellent."

ELEVEN

"S HE'S NOT NINETEEN?" CANDACE ALMOST SHRIEKED and then, remembering that she had just put Brianna to bed, dropped her voice to a stage whisper. "Pierce, surely you can find someone who's closer to your age."

"I did once."

"So you think by robbing the cradle, you are going to avoid being dumped again? What are you going to do? Give her a lollipop each time she says she loves you? Train her your way?"

"Look, Candi, all I know is that Julia is the first woman—"

"You mean *girl,* don't you?"

"Female, then, whom I've been able to talk to since Diane. I just want to get to know her better. Hey! She might think I'm some old boring guy and never want to come over again."

"So I'm just going to call her to come over when we go to the beach and then watch to make sure you two conduct yourself with utmost decorum?"

"And only when I come down for weekends. Make sure she stays for dinner, too. That's no skin off your nose. Gina does the cooking."

Pierce's sister Catherine was even more reticent to play chaperone. "She's closer to Jordan's age than yours, Pierce. What if he has a crush on her? You'll become your nephew's romantic rival!" But she too eventually agreed. They soon discovered Julia was almost impossible not to like. She was observant and quick to pick up on other people's skills, to compliment without being obsequious, to try whatever they were doing: soccer (Jordan), constructing elaborate sand sculptures (Josie), doing little girls' hair (Candace and Brianna), appreciating opera (Catherine). Thus, that first summer, Pierce spent a total of nine weekends with her, and Julia came to consider her new neighbors her friends.

When Julia returned to Harvard in September, Pierce began to text her every morning as his mother had done with him when he was away at law school (without including the "Love You," of course.) One night Julia called him and asked him to "just listen" to her essay on a take-home econ final. "Don't tell me if I'm wrong. Just tell me if my explanation makes sense and if I'm using enough terminology." They talked, usually for a half-of-an-hour on Sundays, and she would ask about his week, and from her questions, he could tell she was listening and was learning enough to find his career interesting. The summer between Julia's sophomore and junior year was a repeat of the previous one, except she would join him when he went running along the beach (she was a much better sprinter than he), and she read some of the same books he was reading (*Quiet: The Power of Introverts in a World That Can't Stop Talking, Salt Sugar Fat: How the Food Giants Hooked Us)*. Intelligent debate had been one of his favorite aspects of his relationship with Diane, and while Julia was not quite as perceptive or opinionated, Pierce reminded himself she was, after all, younger and he liked how the books gave them something substantial to discuss during their walks along the shore.

Three events made Julia's junior year more notable than her first two, from Pierce's perspective. First, a week before New Year's Eve, Loren Cappell called him to see if he was going to the party at the Metropolitan Club. If Pierce would be in attendance, Loren would bring Julia along with him and his wife, Patricia. It was the first time Pierce met Julia's mother, and based on the way she studied his every move—he could feel her eyes literally boring into him—he deduced the Senator had filled her in on their conversation of eighteen months prior. More importantly, Julia and he were on the dance floor all night. (His skill noticeably improved with practice and actual tunes.) He liked the way Julia shone in light blue velvet, surrounded by all the black tuxedos, a rich jewel in the night, much like the diamond earrings dangling against her smooth cheeks. He had guided her to a corner when the countdown to midnight began. Amid the confusion of well-wishing and confetti and balloons, he pulled her close and pressed his lips against hers. It was the first time he ever kissed her. If Cappell saw, he did not regard a holiday buss an offense egregious enough to call for 40 lashes.

Something much more significant occurred in February, though, when Pierce was again Julia's escort, this time to the annual gala that was one of the most notable charity events in New York City. His own parents attended the soiree, as they had for years, to help raise money for Patricia Cappell's Foundation for Pregnancy Loss, Stillbirth and Sudden Infant Death Awareness. It was clearly an evening when Patricia's star shone brighter than her famous husband's. Resplendent in a striking lavender gown, she took the microphone after dinner, and in a voice tinged with just enough pathos, shared with her three hundred or so guests (who had each paid $1000 to be there) how for her, the Foundation was intensely personal. "Loren and I often wondered what cosmic forces were against us, when, after two miscarriages, we found our first child, Elinor, dead one morning in her crib. Two years later, only a month before our son was due to be born, my doctor informed us that she could no longer detect a fetal heartbeat, and Vincent Loren Cappell was delivered, stillborn the next day." Pierce reached for Julia's hand under the table. "The earth swallowed four of our children, but my hope is that their deaths have not been in vain. The foundation they have inspired has helped over a thousand women this year alone to heal, to hope, and to have the courage to face another day. Thank you for your generosity that makes this all possible." Pierce squeezed Julia's hand before she withdrew it to join in the thunderous applause.

Soon after, the other couples who had been seated with Pierce and Julia left for the bar, to dance, or to take part in the silent auction. Once again holding hands surreptitiously, Pierce asked, "Does it bother you when your mother talks about the past?"

Julia shrugged slightly. "No. This is who she is, what she does. She became a crusader before she became my mother, and she does the first extremely well."

"Where do you fit in to that list of children?"

"I was born three years after Vincent. Mother was so afraid she'd lose me too, she didn't even tell Daddy she was pregnant until she was almost six months along."

"Why didn't she mention you tonight?"

"She never does. People donate more if they feel sorry for her for having four babies that died, not one that lived."

Looking at Julia's bright eyes, and hearing her speak of Patricia Cappell, without the least trace of anger or resentment, an awareness that he was starting to love her crept into Pierce's consciousness. He wanted to hold her close, to let her know that to him, she was going to become the most important person in the world—the sun, moon and stars. But there were reporters in attendance, and he did not want his embracing Julia to become merely fodder for the society pages or to anger Cappell, so instead Pierce led Julia to the dance floor where his holding her was less conspicuous. "You do realize that every eye in this room is looking at you," he whispered in her ear just as the big band orchestra began to play their rendition of the 80's classic "Take My Breath Away." Pierce followed Julia's eyes as she scanned the ballroom, and a faint blush painted her cheeks when she saw that he was speaking the truth. He pulled her closer. "When all these people donate tonight, I assure you it will be because they have seen what beautiful, intelligent children Patricia and Loren must have lost."

However, the most important incident of that year occurred two days later: Pierce realized he had gone for forty-eight hours without thinking once of Diane. Diane's floating blonde beauty was finally fading, especially as Julia became more integrated into his world, a permanent fixture and less of an ornament to see and admire on trips to Martha's Vineyard.

That summer, Senator Cappell decided with Julia's graduation only a year away, it was high time for her to learn more about running his real estate enterprise instead of spending the majority of June, July and August at the beach. Julia looked forward to the challenge; the majority of their conversations the preceding April and May had been about the need they both felt to prove themselves, to squelch all accusations of nepotism, to earn the genuine respect of their parents' employees. Now that Julia was working the same long hours he was, Pierce would call her at 9:00 each night throughout the week, often just as she was arriving home, and they would talk about the deals she had been part of, the cost of renovations to properties; she asked him pointed questions about some of the language of the contracts sitting on her desk.

Pierce had also been given permission to take Julia out to dinner on Saturdays, but only at restaurants that had earned the Senator's approval.

Cappell also sanctioned their attending a couple Broadway shows. (Pierce selected the ones that featured the most dancing.) On Saturdays, if the Yankees were in town, they went to the stadium. (She quickly learned to identify a curveball and how to keep score.) Pierce also secured permission to take her to several of the city's museums, which was how they frequently spent Sunday afternoons. One such excursion in August led them to Brooklyn Botanical's Japanese Hill-and-Pond Garden, where Julia turned into a picture-taking fiend, a side of her he had never seen before. "You didn't know I love flowers?" she said as she zoomed in for a close up of some magenta blossoms. "I thought I told you how they were one of my favorite parts of my dance recitals."

"What kind of flowers did your legions of admirers send you?"

"Don't tease me. You know they always came from my parents, and Daddy always sent lilies."

"Not roses?"

"He said roses are only for lovers, and that lilies smelled just as sweet."

Monday morning, Pierce called the florist in Cambridge. When Julia returned to Harvard for her senior year, a single rose was delivered to her every day. The card simply read "Pierce." He would allow her to infer the rest from the language of flowers.

TWELVE

S HORTLY AFTER JULIA FINISHED HER STINT working for her father, Senator Cappell arranged to meet Pierce, again for dinner at the Metropolitan. The young man had proven himself a gentleman, never crossing the line with his daughter. He knew they were seen holding hands at the theater, and Pierce sometimes draped his arm across Julia's shoulder at the ball park, but that was to be expected. His daughter was a beautiful girl, and if Pierce hadn't expressed any physical affection for her, that too would be a cause for concern. Supremely hard for a man like Pierce in the prime of life to wait for a woman. No wonder he distracted himself by working, usually seventy hours a week, turning the insurance division into the most profitable part of his family's company.

"I want to run a few ideas past you," Cappell told Pierce over drinks. "First, the fact that you're sending Julia roses every day, from what I've heard, would indicate that you're truly interested in marrying her."

"I am."

Cappell liked the way Pierce said it. He was used to yes-men because the people he dealt with for the most part understood that Loren Cappell typically got his way, and it was better to acquiesce, and say "I will, I do," rather than wage a futile fight. But he had also learned to listen to how the words were said. Men could talk out both sides of their mouth, say "yes" and then try to stab him in the back. Pierce's sincerity was palpable.

"Then, if that's the case, Tricia and I would like you to join us for Christmas. We're going to spend it in Switzerland, skiing."

Pierce lifted his forehead in good-natured discomfiture and took a swallow of his club soda before replying, "I don't ski, or at least I haven't since, I think I was maybe nine? After that, I was so into baseball, I was afraid of breaking something, and when my pitching career was over—let's just say I didn't want to be on the bunny hill when I was 20."

"I don't ski myself, so this is not some sort of test on my part. It's not like I'm going to rescind my permission for you to marry my daughter if you can't race down a double black diamond in world class time. Skiing is just something Tricia and Julia like and both are pretty good."

Cappell could see Pierce was a little relieved as he replied, "My mother has always insisted the family celebrate Christmas together on Christmas Eve, but—I'll need to check a few items on my schedule—I should be able to fly out on the 25th and join you for a few days."

"Great. I can appreciate the requirement to put family first. Julia says your sisters are great girls." Loren leaned back. "Now for the second idea: when Julia graduates in June, she's naturally going to come to work for me so I can groom her to take over the whole shebang someday if I ever decide to retire. She did a superlative job this summer, proved she deserves to be there because of what she can do, not just because she's my daughter. You can probably relate. I'd like a time frame, though, on when you are going to propose."

Again, no hesitation, completely open—honest: "I was thinking around her birthday. I don't want to compete with a Harvard graduation."

"Great." (The adjective was Cappell's favorite.) I'll tell Tricia to plan on an engagement party, Labor Day Weekend."

Pierce left the Metropolitan relieved, contented, suffused in joy. It was settled, then. He could marry Julia and luxuriate in the sure prospect of her soon becoming his wife. Their happiness, just as Diane had predicted, would rest on the security of their families' wealth, the certainty that there were few couples more alike in background, intelligence, and even pulchritude. Pierce only wished that July 31st, Julia's twenty-second birthday, were tomorrow.

THIRTEEN

B Y THE TIME PIERCE ARRIVED IN St. Moritz, given the time change, it was mid-morning, the day after Christmas. Julia was waiting for him in the lobby of the five-star Kempinski. Even though Pierce knew by now that he was probably in Cappell's sights, he kissed Julia . . . and then again because she asked him to. "You should most definitely write a book about your technique."

She also suggested that he take a nap ("I know trying to sleep on a plane is brutal!"), but Pierce knew that he was too excited, too anxious to rest, and within the hour, they were headed to the slopes. "Okay, you need to remember that while I do possess sundry talents, skiing is not one of them."

"You did fine the weekend we went with your nieces," she reassured him.

He had taken his sisters, Brianna and Josie skiing in upstate New York over Thanksgiving, and Julia had joined them. Actually, he had been pretty pleased with his ability to remain upright, to schuss; the concept of stopping, however, had eluded him until his tenth run. "Showing up a seven year old on a green circle slope is not something I brag about."

She kissed him on the cheek. "We'll go slow."

"If I hurt myself, will you take care of me?"

"Oh yes."

The overtly suggestive innuendo of her reply was one of Pierce's favorite memories of the trip. That, and how the last day, as they rode in the lift to the top of the *Paradiso piste*, she had gazed at the snow-covered Alps sparkling under the blue ski, totally delighted. "Winter is so beautiful. I've always wanted to get married in winter, dressed in fur, even though that's no longer politically correct, and then go skiing on my honey moon."

How much had Daddy Cappell told her about his plans? Pierce decided the most appropriate response would be "Noted."

When they reached the top, Pierce told Julia to go ahead, he would be fine, and then followed her down the *piste*, admiring her grace, the trimness of her form, the sheen of her dark hair billowing behind her. Only seven months more until he would place his grandmother's two carat marquis-cut diamond on her finger. If she wanted to be married in the winter, he hoped Cappell would agree to a short engagement, and then it would be only a year until he could call her "Mine."

Pierce's sense of anticipation overwhelmed him as the winter limped into spring. There was the sensual delight of being in Julia's presence when she surprised him on his birthday in April, just as he was leaving the office. (Her gift: a studio portrait of herself, only her upturned face and shoulders visible, photographed from above, so that she was looking up as if she were emerging from an enormous bouquet of roses.) For the first time, she invited him to the Eliot House's elaborate Spring Fete, where she so clearly surpassed every other woman there. It was not just her beauty, but her class, her sophistication, her maturity. He marveled at her poise during their now daily conversations, the woman she had become in the four years he had known her. He took comfort in ticking off each day that passed; only one week now, until her graduation, and then he could say, "Next month, I'll be engaged." He called the jeweler and made arrangements to have his grandmother's ring sized. When he ordered the flowers for her graduation, he included a hand-written card: *Today the president will give you your diploma, and I give you all my love. Pierce.*

When Pierce woke from his restless sleep at half past ten, he opened the file of photos on his phone to peruse them again. Pierce had taken very few pictures of Julia because of Cappell's stringent rules for dating Julia. (Sometimes Pierce had felt like Julia's father wanted his daughter to be on a tether that he could pull back, so unwilling was he to give her any liberty.) There were a few from St. Moritz, the Fete—the first photos which captured the fact they were now more than just friends. But Cappell, who sat to Pierce's left at Commencement, was snapping pictures of his *magna*

cum laude daughter himself, and said nothing when Pierce pulled out his phone and joined in. In every single one, Julia was smiling. Her eyes were shining. The last image was a shot of them together, his arms around her waist, her hand resting on his chest. What had happened in one short week? The woman whom he had come to think of as his future wife, his bride, "the fabulous woman from his own *milieu* who made him very happy and loved him for himself alone"? He wondered what Dr. Shaelyn K. Speare would discover.

FOURTEEN

T HE WORD "COLD" WAS FREQUENTLY USED to describe Patricia Cappell. The fact that she and her husband Loren often spent weeks apart led to rampant speculation about the happiness of her marriage. Many considered her "difficult." She was notoriously critical, impatient and demanding. However, her detractors did not include Angelica Nurre, who had raised Patricia Cappell's daughter.

Angelica had married her high school sweet heart Austin right before he shipped out for Japan to serve out his deployment with the Marines. Their weekend honeymoon in the Poconos left Angelica pregnant. She was thrilled when the sonogram revealed it would be a girl. She displayed the picture of her "daughter" in the clear plastic sleeve she wore from a lanyard around her neck. The customers of the ShopRite where she checked out groceries were treated to an account of her pregnancy that was far from refined. ("I barfed every time I got in a car for the first three months . . . Oh God! That pastrami is, like, the thing I am *so* craving today! . . . This heartburn just sucks! . . . I am going to have to pee *again* as soon as I finish with you.") When Angelica's water broke two weeks before her due date, just as she was placing two gallons of milk in a customer's cart, her expletive resounded down every aisle.

Angelica had been very close to her "Nana Susan," who had died of cancer two days after attending Angelica's high school graduation. ("She stayed alive just to make damn sure I graduated!") For Angelica, the only possible name for her beloved baby girl was "Susan." On July 30, Susan was born at 11:59. ("Guess she arrived in time to party at mid-night!").

Marine Corps privates serving overseas don't make much money, and Angelica returned to ShopRite within a few weeks, to the congratulations of her regular customers, who were now treated to uncensored accounts of Susan's bowel movements and breastfeeding. Such accounts gave Angelica's register "local color" and for many were part of the charm of their food shopping experience, which is why, after a few days of her absence, they asked about her.

ShopRite customers would never see Angelica again. She could not face them, could not bear the prospect of their questions about Susan, who, one morning had not woken Angelica up with her cries demanding a 3:00 A.M. feeding. "Good girl, letting Mommy finally sleep." Angelica would forever rue the fact that she had not rolled out of bed to check on her baby girl. When Angelica did over go to the crib a little after 6:00, Susan was cold and limp. Angelica's hysterical shrieks woke the sleeping neighbors.

Angelica was inconsolable. Two friends of Austin's who had played football with him had to hold her back when the funeral director insisted on closing the lid to Baby Susan's small white coffin. The minister conducting the funeral was barely audible over her moans and sobbing. The burial at the cemetery was ungodly, as Angelica reached down in the grave and tried to retrieve the casket, maniacally repeating "No!" until she fell into stupor. For the next twenty four hours, she huddled on her bed, holding her leaking breasts, and wept as she stared at Susan's empty crib. She did not eat; she did not drink. She vowed to die with her infant daughter.

Austin appeared the next day, having received an emergency leave. When his devastation did not match her own, Angelica pronounced him a "Bastard," screamed that she never wanted to see him again, and threw every loose item in her room—diapers, pillows, lamps—in his direction until he left, never to return. The first time Angelica slept was four days later, after she drank a six pack of beer in little over an hour.

Her mother knew Angelica needed help. The obstetrician gave her a prescription for anti-depressants, which she refused to take. "Angelica needs counseling." Mental health services were expensive, and Austin had already filed papers for a separation, so she was uninsured. A friend searched the web, and found out about the Cappell Foundation for Pregnancy Loss, Stillbirth and Sudden Infant Death Awareness. Angelica would later say it saved her life.

How she ended up in one of the Foundation's offices one month later, Angelica could not recall. But she would always remember how Patricia, who was inspecting that particular office that day, had consoled her. They spoke in a back room for nearly two hours about Susan and Elinor and Vincent. Angelica found in Patricia a kindred soul, someone who could truly share her pain and who was willing to hold her and weep with her. Thus, whenever a comment was made about Patricia Cappell's uptight, rigid manner, Angelica would share the account of her first encounter, including the detail that "there was like my snot and tears all over Patricia's silk sweater, and it didn't even faze her! Uptight? My butt!"

It took a long time, but Angelica was eventually able to function normally again. Now divorced and unemployed, Angelica was hired by Patricia Cappell to work as a receptionist for the Foundation. A little over a year later, Patricia had come to the office at closing time. She explained that she was unhappy with her daughter Julia's foreign nanny. Would Angelica consider such a position?

"So Patricia takes me to their penthouse, and I'm, like riding in this elevator that was something like in those movies. Their living room is sunken and has all these fancy rugs and there are all these sky lights and windows everywhere. And she takes me back to this bedroom where there was the prettiest baby. She was able to stand, but wasn't real steady yet, and she went down—BAM! —and started to cry. I just picked her up and fell in love. Later, I found out that she and my Susan were born not even a day apart. And from that moment on, Julia Cappell has been like my own daughter."

Angelica soon called her new charge Ju Ju Bean. Rather than commute into mid-town Manhattan, she was given a room at the Cappells. Both parents worked long hours; Loren Cappell traveled extensively, so it was Angelica who fed Ju Ju Bean, bathed her, played with her and adored her. The Cappells were fastidious about enrolling their only child in the right pre-schools. ("Can you believe they *interview* the kids for Pete's sake? I mean a toddler going on an interview!") But it was Angelica who dropped Julia off and picked her up, and took her to Suzuki lessons and monitored her practice on her miniature violin. She quickly realized that Julia much preferred dance class ("And when she comes out in that little tutu and her hair up in a bow, I could just eat her up!"). Since it did not fit into Patricia's schedule, it was also Angelica who stood in the pool during Mommy and Me swim class, her arms out-stretched to encourage a hesitant Ju Ju to jump in.

Once Angelica's mother observed, "You would think, as rich as they are, that Patricia would stay home with Julia, now that she finally has a child."

Angelica had risen to her feet, full of indignation. "Don't you *dare* criticize her! You don't know what she's been through!" Yet, privately, Angelica had often asked herself the same question. Angelica sensed, though, with an intuition born from them both having daughters on virtually the same day, and from both finding a baby girl dead in her crib, that Patricia Cappell was afraid of her precious daughter. Afraid that if she loved Julia too much, Fate would whisk her away. Afraid that it was some deficiency in herself that had led to four unfulfilled pregnancies. Afraid that she was perhaps, on an even cellular level, an unfit mother. Fortunately, Patricia Cappell had found Angelica, who rescinded her vow to die with Susan and instead vowed to love Julia enough for both of them.

FIFTEEN

W HEN JULIA STARTED SCHOOL FULL TIME, and Angelica's child-care duties were reduced to conducting Julia to and from school, monitoring her homework, and taking her to dance classes, Angelica transitioned into the housekeeper and even, at times, the cook, especially when Loren and Patricia were out of town. Angelica's constant presence, her easy proximity, and availability made her the Mom, and Patricia remained the formal woman whom Julia respected as Mother. During Julia's teenage years, Patricia set the rules for the clothes Julia could wear, how much make-up was permitted, what hairstyles were acceptable. But it was Angelica who took Julia (no longer Ju Ju Bean, but "Sweetie) shopping, helped her select her outfits on the days when the girls at Julia's exclusive all-female academy were given a reprieve from uniforms, who taught Julia how to apply eye-liner, and who arranged her hair in an up-do for dance class.

As Julia matured, Loren became intensively protective. His status warranted some of his precautions, and knowing the media spotlight could be unpleasant, he was overzealous in shielding Julia from its glare. In Angelica's mind, poor Julia was lonely, and she feared Julia would be dangerously naïve, since she was forbidden to date or have a boyfriend. If asked, she even had to provide an explanation for any boy she contacted—and Loren had people who checked out his daughter's calls. Angelica, recalling her own raucous teenage years, considered it a miracle that Julia did not rebel. However, for Julia, her parents' restrictions were a fact of existence, as much a given as her need for oxygen or water.

Naturally, it was Angelica who told her about sex and—the bastard Austin aside—men. "It's when they're boys that they're most dangerous because they never *think*. They just *do*. But once they grow up, Sweetie, not all men are liars and not all of them are out to use you for a good time. It seems to me that there's an island of good men out there, and occasionally, a few of them escape. The trick, of course, is to find one."

"How can I tell if I've found one?" Julia asked, sitting on the bed in Angelica's room as Angelica painted Julia's toenails a Patricia-sanctioned shade of pink.

"You remember that statue of *David* you included in your slides for that presentation on Michelangelo?"

"The one you said had the best butt you'd ever seen?"

"That's the one, Sweetie." Angelica dipped the brush back in the bottle. "The perfect man will look like that. And when he kisses you for the first time, he'll take your breath away. But what's most important, he'll always let you know that *you* are in charge, and that *you* call the shots," Angelica wiped away the excess, "cause if he doesn't and hurts my girl, he'll have to deal with me."

"Daddy's already told me he'll whip and starve any boy who does anything to me that he wouldn't do in front of Daddy."

"Sweetie," Angelica capped the polish, and blew gently on Julia's toes, "if the best that your Daddy can do is starve the boy who hurts my Julia, then I will make your daddy look like a worn-out dishcloth."

A week or so after Julia's high school graduation, Angelica and Julia took a road trip to Massachusetts, their first stop: Harvard. "I want to be able to *see* in my mind where you are when you call me, and you better call or text each day so I know you are okay." She posed Julia in front of Widener Library, Memorial Church, before the statue of John Harvard. They ate a picnic along the Charles, and inspected her dormitory (more pictures.) Then Angelica drove her up to Martha's Vineyard, where Loren had recently purchased a new summer home. He reasoned that his daughter should try to become a little more independent before she started college life, and in contrast to his Manhattan penthouse, an island seemed safer. With Julia gone, Angelica would start a new job at the Foundation but could join Julia on weekends. Angelica stayed a few days once she was sure the housekeeper was competent and then cried the entire way back to New York.

Angelica first heard about Pierce in a text from Julia, to the effect that, by not coming to Martha's Vineyard for just one weekend, Angelica had missed out on meeting a reasonable David facsimile. The next summer, Angelica only came down a couple weekends because she required extensive dental work. (Her periodontist at one point declared she was at risk of having only four teeth left.) But Julia did send her a picture of Pierce on the beach, and Angelica quickly agreed he shared several features of the famous Michelangelo sculpture—although Pierce had better hair. "Do you have a bit of a crush on him?" she asked Julia when she called her that night.

"Ang, he's so much older than me! His sisters and their kids are just really nice and probably think it must be lonely for me to be here by myself."

Pierce's daily text messages when Julia returned to college for her second year had sent JuJu over the moon. "They don't always come in at the same time, so I know they're not automatic either. Just a reminder to have a good day. You don't think he likes me or something, do you?"

"Everybody who meets you likes you, Sweetie." But now Angelica wanted to meet this Pierce. Her pretty baby had grown into a stunning woman, and to be honest, Angelica feared Pierce might just be another rich man on the look-out for arm candy that would advertise his status.

Thus the following summer, Angelica purposely drove over for the first weekend Pierce was supposed to be there just to meet him. Her first reaction: the picture that Julia had sent did not do his eyes justice; they were green, not gray. He was also polite—didn't dismiss her as mere servant like some of the hoity-toities—made effortless small talk about the Foundation, found out she lived in Brooklyn now, and apologized when he realized he had digressed for several minutes into Dodgers baseball history. She asked him to lunch, and he complimented her baked chicken sandwiches.

But it was his interactions with Julia that held Angelica's attention the most. Something about them reminded Angelica of how she had felt one time when Nana Susan had bought her this to-die-for white dress with flowers embroidered on it, and a full skirt that flared out when she twirled. Angelica had wanted to wear it right then, but Nana said she must wait until her cousin's wedding. Angelica realized Pierce, no matter how crazy he was about Julia, had clearly been told he must wait until the wedding, too.

The summer after that, Julia worked for her father, so Angelica saw her more because she came by early most mornings to make Julia breakfast. "Still think he is too old for you?" she asked Julia one morning, having listened to an account of their weekend together while scrambling eggs with Swiss cheese, Julia's favorite.

"You're the one who said *boys* were the problems." Julia waited for Angelica to sit down, and as Angelica slid a plate in front of her, added, "I like the fact that he is *mature*, that he's established in his career. I don't have to wonder how he'll turn out. I already know."

"So what's it like when he kisses you?"

Julia played with her eggs at the end of her fork. "The first time was on midnight New Year's Eve, but in St. Moritz—"

"Well, don't leave me in suspense. Did he take your breath away?"

"I was able to breathe. I just didn't want him to stop."

Angelica poured her coffee. "You'll finish college next year, Sweetie, and something tells me your graduation present from him is going to be a big, beautiful diamond. I'll bet every last one of my teeth on it."

The daily rose, though, in Angelica's mind, was the ultimate proof of Pierce's honorable intentions. "Are they always the same color?" she asked, when Julia called for her daily check in.

"They started out white, and this week they're pink."

"Next week will be red," Angelica predicted.

The morning of Julia's college graduation, Angelica had come by Julia's room to help her dress and take pictures. Patricia and Loren would be at the ceremony, and there, Angelica would let them claim parental honors. But in private moments like these, JuJu was still hers. A knock on the door. "Get that, would you please Ang?" The doorframe was suddenly filled with two dozen Harvard Crimson roses that Pierce had sent. "Ang! He signed it all his *love!*"

At the ceremony in Harvard Yard, surrounded by males a decade younger, Angelica decided Pierce somehow *did* seem more desirable. (Some still had pimples, for Pete's sake!) Few could match him when it came to looks—he literally did turn several female heads—but even more he exuded a confidence, a masculine elegance that was deeper than just his cologne or Armani blazer or the amount in his checking account. Pierce, by waiting, had proven to her that his was a gentleman-like offer. He *deserved* Julia, and he had Angelica's blessing.

SIXTEEN

The day before Rome Ayo's death

So convinced was Angelica that Pierce would propose the day of graduation, she stayed up until 3:00 A.M. waiting for a text, a call, or a picture of the ring. The next day, Friday, when she had not heard from Julia, she sent a text: *What's going on?* Perhaps Pierce had finally . . . God forgive her for actually hoping.

Saturday morning, around 6:30 A.M., she woke to frantic pounding on her apartment door. It was Julia.

She was dressed, but her jeans and shirt—more low-cut than anything Angelica had ever seen—even her sandals all seemed to have been thrown on. Her mascara had started to run. She was crying.

"Sweetie, what is it? Tell Angie. Shhh, JuJu." She held Julia's trembling body close to hers. "Is it Pierce?"

Julia could only shake her head, until she finally hiccoughed, "He can't know I'm here. She pulled out her phone and turned it off. "Turn your phone off, too, Ang."

Angelica walked back to her bedroom to retrieve it and returned, holding the blank screen so that Julia could see it was off. Something was terribly wrong. Julia stumbled to the couch, where she curled up in fetal position in the corner. Angelica was scared. "Julia, you better tell me what's going on."

"I can't."

"You will, or, or—I'll call your father."

"Ty said I had to keep quiet."

"You can tell *me* anything. Now out with it!" Angelica tucked an afghan around Julia's shivering form and knelt on the floor before her.

"He raped me, I'm pretty sure, but I can't *remember*. Ty says he probably drugged my drink. And then when I woke up, I was in some bedroom, and there was a light on in the bathroom. I had trouble walking, but I made it, and he was in there," a huge gasp, "dead." Julia literally rocked back and forth. "Ang, how does a good girl like *me* end up in a situation like *this*?"

Angelica felt as though she were being suffocated but as much by confusion as rage. "Who raped you?" She was surprised by how calm her voice sounded, especially since she already knew what she must do next. "I'll kill him."

"You can't."

"I most certainly can and will. Who did this to you? Pierce?"

"How can you say such a thing? Pierce would *never—!*" A look of sheer panic and Julia clutched Angelica's arm. "Pierce doesn't know anything. And he can't. He mustn't."

"Then who hurt you, Sweetie?"

A barely audible whisper: "His name is Rome Ayo.'

"That singer?" A nod to confirm.

"Then who's dead, JuJu? I don't understand. Talk to me."

"Rome."

"Rome raped you, then *died*?"

"Yes."

"Where?"

"My cousin Ty's club. The Vault." Julia took several deep breaths. "Ty told me he'd take care of things but I didn't know where to go. I had him bring me here."

"The wisest thing that wild boy has ever done." Angelica reached out, and Julia came to snuggle against her, and Angelica cuddled her close as she had when Julia was little and frightened by a bad dream. "You know Ang will take care of you." But at the same time, Angelica realized she had no clue as to what to do next. The man she needed to kill to avenge her beloved Julia was already dead.

SEVENTEEN

Ty Katz could legitimately claim he had connections. His uncle—okay, by marriage to his Aunt Tricia—was Loren Freaking Cappell, who had helped him find the space for his club and had endorsed his idea that celebrities would pay top dollar to party without the risk of being photographed by *paparazzi*. Of course, his uncle had flipped when he heard that Ty's clients were smoking weed and snorting coke, and taking advantage of Ty's policy that anything done in The Vault never made it past its walls. But celebrity clients loved it: the fact a nondescript car tricked out with a luxury interior and tinted windows would drop them off at the covered walkway entrance for the best food, booze, and music in the City, all provided with the utmost discretion. Ty was rolling in major buckage by the time Uncle Loren decided to run for Senator and turned all moral in order to grub a few extra votes from pious church-types. When Cappell paid a quick visit to Ty between Senate campaign appearances, he called his nephew a few choice names and pitched a fit about his ingratitude, threatening to call his loan. Ty paid it off in full and told his Uncle Cappell to go screw himself.

This dysfunctional family situation meant that he had not seen his cousin Julia since she was in junior high. In fact, he was surprised when she had called him and asked if she could come to New York to celebrate her graduation. Not that he was perverted or anything, but hey, she was even hotter than he remembered when she strolled into his club on Friday night a little after ten, in painted-on jeans and a top that left nothing to the imagination. She knew how to walk in her high heels, too. A shimmy and shake on the dance floor, and he remembered she was a dancer. (Once, years ago, he had even been forced to attend one of her recitals.)

Surprise, surprise. It was Rome Ayo who noticed her about two seconds later. Cocky. Full of himself, especially now that he'd won that Grammy. Always switching his women, like they were flavors of the day. Easy to tell with Rome which girl he was going to chase: the prettiest face in the room. Friday night, it was Julia.

Because Ty's clients loved that nothing embarrassing would ever be leaked to the press and that Ty could take care of every situation without any back up from the police, they all agreed to sign a contract releasing Ty, his heirs, and about twenty thousand other parties from indemnity or liability for their behaviors. (His top-flight attorneys had made that clause airtight.) Obviously, there were no surveillance cameras at The Vault, so Ty had to be on constant alert to prevent problems before they started. Ty and his two security men (KGB wannabees) maintained control by always making the rounds, diffusing issues with humor, free drinks, flattery, and occasionally a little force. At all times, they knew who was high, who was drunk, who was headed to the suites upstairs and in what condition.

Rome and Julia were at the bar, but before Ty finished his first round, Rome flashed him the key to the suite with a hot tub. Ty knew what would transpire—it was so predictable—and there was a moment of impulse to protect his cousin, but Ty reasoned Julia was an adult and Rome was *People* magazine's Sexiest Man Alive. She was probably more than willing. Ty looked at the time. Rome was working fast tonight. Not even 10:30.

Six hours later, most of the clients had been driven back to their homes or hotels, or had decided to crash in one of his $400-a-night rooms upstairs; Ty was just starting to let his guard down. His phone vibrated; he recognized the number of Rome's suite. "Hey."

It was Julia, not Rome. "Ty, you need to get up her right away." He could tell by her voice she was totally freaked out.

Ty took the steps two at a time and knocked once. The door opened just a crack, and he pushed it wide. He found a dark room and Julia wrapped in a sheet, sitting on the edge of the bed. She nodded in the direction of the bathroom, where the light was on. In the adjoining room, where the hot tub was still bubbling, he found Rome Ayo's body. Many expletives. Cold fear thrills that Rome Ayo's lawyers might be better than his, and Ty's gold mine would collapse.

Ty was mindful not to touch anything. His mind was working at lightning speed. First, deal with Julia. He returned to the bedroom. "What happened?" He tried to sound cool. She was in no shape for a slap-down interrogation.

"No idea. I can't remember anything."

"You were at the bar. Do you remember that? I saw you. Do you remember what you ordered?"

Julia shook her head. "I told your bartender to surprise me."

"How much did you drink?"

She shrugged. "It was awful; maybe a couple swallows. I don't like the taste of liquor."

Ty braced himself for what she might say next. "It was around 10:30 when I saw you leave with Rome. That was over six hours ago. What have you been doing since then?"

"I don't know. Sleeping?"

Ty turned on the light and looked at the bed. Blood. Of course Uncle Loren's daughter would be a virgin. He knew it was violating The Vault's preserve-celebrity-secrets policy, but he also knew that it might be in his best interest to have some blackmail power should Ayo's attorney threaten some legal action, so he asked anyway: "Julia, if I take you to the hospital, will you let them do a rape kit?"

"*What?*" A total meltdown. Screw it. He had no time and he was facing a much bigger problem. He gripped her bare shoulders and shook her. "Listen to me! Are you listening? I'm going to make you repeat everything I say so you had better be listening!"

"I'm listening." She sounded stoned—or scared.

"I think Rome spiked your drink with ruffies." Her quizzical expression made him explain: "It's a sedative that causes amnesia, a date rape drug that would explain why you can't remember anything. It looks like he," Ty paused for a less blunt term to avoid another hissy fit, "took full advantage of you. Without a rape kit, you'll never know." Silently, Ty cursed her womanish tears. He gripped her shoulders and gave her a shake. "Julia, I'm sorry about what happened. But we've got a bigger problem: Rome is freaking dead in that hot tub." He paused so that the impact of his words would register and his gut reactions could take shape and become a plan. "Here's what I am going to do. I am going to clean everything but that room. I'll say that when I came in, I thought Rome was gone, I cleaned it, and then when I went to sanitize the hot tub, found him. I will wipe down everything, wash the sheets. No one will ever know you were even in here."

She was not stupid. Hey, she'd gone to Harvard and could put two and two together. "It looks like I killed him, doesn't it?"

"I saw a bottle. I bet he got drunk, turned the hot tub too high and stayed in it too long because he was too bombed to realize he was boiling his brains. Get dressed. Is there somewhere you can go besides Uncle Loren's?"

It was already light when, after an almost wordless drive in one of the club's decoy cars—a grey Toyota—Ty pulled up in front of Angelica's apartment in Brooklyn with a final admonition: "I'll make it all go away Julia, but you have to keep your mouth shut." He watched, to make sure Julia was inside, and then pulled away from the curb. Thank God it was still so early; the birds were still singing to herald the morning. The only person out on the street was someone walking a Cocker spaniel. Ty pulled away from the curb and was careful not to speed; he could not risk getting pulled over. Too freaking much to do.

EIGHTEEN

Shaelyn Speare leaned over Julia's bed and then took Julia's two hands in her own as her patient's eyes fluttered open. "Good morning, Julia." Shae modulated her voice so that it was gentle, warm, and soothing yet authentic and not condescending. "I'm Dr. Shaelyn Speare, and you are in a hospital. You tried to hurt yourself, but right now you are safe. We won't let anyone hurt you. Our only job is to help you. You'll let us do that, won't you?" She waited for an acknowledgement: a perceptible nod. "My nurses are going to take care of you. Until we know you are all right, they will have to stay close to you at all times. They do have some clothes that you'll find a little more stylish than that hospital gown, so if you want, get ready, and then we'll talk, maybe eat some breakfast if you like. Do you have any questions?"

Julia's eyes scanned the light blue walls (the shade of paint had been carefully selected for its calming effect). They seemed to linger at the window, as if she were trying to ascertain the time of day from the sunlight. Still groggy from the sedation, Julia murmured, "How did I get here?"

"An ambulance brought you from the City early this morning."

Bending her arm to adjust the blanket, Julia noticed the white gauze wrapped around her wrist. She swallowed hard and bit her lower lip. Tears beaded the corners of her eyes, but she won the struggle to maintain her composure. With barely a catch in her voice, she managed to inquire, "Is Angelica here?"

"No." Dr. Speare waited, wondering if Julia would ask for Pierce. When she did not, Dr. Speare motioned to the nurses, introducing them. "This is Samantha, and this is Gracy." Sam peeked out from the bathroom where she had started the shower and waved. Gracy had already moved forward to remove Julia's IV. Dr. Speare squeezed Julia's hands reassuringly. "I'll be back soon."

Only twenty minutes later, Julia arrived in Dr. Speare's office, clad in a pink designer warm-up, escorted by Gracy. Seated in a deep arm chair, her long dark hair still wet, Julia looked almost like a child or a stranger in an alien world.

Dr. Speare took a seat nearby. Julia was quick to make visual contact. The fact her patient's eyes were not listless or vacant pleased Shae. Instead, they communicated Julia's need to be liked as she even managed a faint smile. Dr. Speare mirrored it before she began: "I really don't want to ask you a bunch of questions, Julia. I'm really more interested in what *you* want to say. Sometimes, people just need to talk, and that's why I'm here, to just listen, no judgments."

Several seconds of silence in these situations were typical, sometimes downright uncomfortable, but Dr. Speare accepted this as normal and waited, careful not to fidget. Finally, Julia shifted in her chair, first stroking the fingers of her right hand against the back of her left until the tips made contact with the bandage. She looked up and then away, before rewarding Dr. Speare by beginning softly, "You know, I took a psychology course in college. Doesn't cutting reveal anger and self-loathing?"

"It can. Do you feel angry?"

"Yes . . ." A tense pause, and then barely audibly, "But only with myself."

Dr. Speare again waited. Time enough to observe Julia's French manicure, her well-proportioned features, the length of her dark lashes. Julia Cappell's beauty did not rely on cosmetics. Dr. Speare's observations were interrupted when Julia asked, in the same whisper, "Is this where we try to figure out if my issues trace back to my childhood?" Julia's attitude was not hostile or sarcastic; she was simply asserting her awareness of the process and her willingness to cooperate with it.

Dr. Speare smiled. "If you want."

Julia continued to stroke the back of her hands, almost meditatively and then, "I know that some people think Daddy is overbearing and that Mother is aloof. But each of them *do* love me, at least in their own way and as much as they can. They've given me everything they could, and probably more. I can't ask for more than that."

"And Angelica?"

Julia leaned back, as if even the name had the power to relax her. "She raised me. She loves me like a daughter, and I think of her as a cross between a mom and a favorite aunt or grandma. That's probably why I thought Ang brought me here. That and I went to her when—everything happened."

"Everything?" Silently, Dr. Speare handed Julia bottle of Fiji water.

"Thanks." Julia unscrewed the cap and took a swallow. A deep cleansing breath and another pause before Julia's words began to unwind slowly, as if she were rehearsing each sentence before uttering it. "It happened last Friday morning. The day before, I had graduated *magna cum laude* from Harvard. Daddy had offered me a job with a starting salary of a quarter million dollars; the man I want to marry told me he loved me. When I woke up, though, after that totally perfect day, I don't know what happened. My heart was racing. I was in a cold sweat. It hurt to breathe. I actually thought I was having a heart attack. So I went to the health clinic, and the doctor checked me out and told me I'd had an anxiety attack, and recommended I see one of their psychiatrists, so I did.

"His name was Dr. Lawrence. We talked, I don't know, maybe a half hour? Basically, he said that I was panicking because all my life, I had been making people happy, doing what was expected of me, and that I was afraid that pleasing others was all I would ever do. What he said seemed logical, and I even agreed he was right. So he suggested I try doing something out of character and see how that felt.

"That's when I called my cousin, Ty. He owns this trendy celebrity nightclub in New York. Daddy absolutely hates it, so it seemed like a perfect place to do something 'out of character.' I stopped and bought some slutty clothes, took the T to Logan and flew into La Guardia. Ty sent a car to meet me, and the driver took me to The Vault. I do remember walking in; it was so *loud*. I liked the song though, so I got out and danced. But other than meeting a guy who was really very cute, and having one drink, I remember *nothing* until I woke up in a room I had never seen." A pause and then wryly: "I seem to be doing that way too often lately."

An attempt at humor was a good sign. Julia ran her fingers through her hair and glanced at Dr. Speare. "What happened next still seems so surreal. The room was dark but there was a light coming from a door that was sort of opened." Julia was now twisting and untwisting her hair around her fingers, more and more quickly as her agitation increased. "I wish I had never gone there." Julia spat the words. "I would gladly deny that I ever went to The Vault, to that room, or through that door. But I did. I didn't have any clothes on, so I wrapped myself in the sheet. I could hear the water in the hot tub before I even walked in. And when I was able to actually see it—the tub—I could just tell that the cute guy . . . yeah, he was in there, and there was just something that let me know he was—dead."

Dr. Speare, pleasantly surprised by how willingly Julia had opened up, was anticipating the excruciating details of a sexual assault, so the corpse—a completely unexpected turn—jarred her. Suddenly aware that her eyebrows had shot up and that her mouth no longer resembled the inscrutable Mona Lisa's, Dr. Speare quickly brought her expression back to one of impassive objectivity. She watched as Julia drew her knees to her chest and clasped her legs, making the bandages on her wrists all the more prominent. "I called Ty on the house phone. He was there almost right away. So much of this is still kind of fuzzy. But I do know he started talking about some date rape drug that starts with an 'R.'"

The longest pause, as Dr. Speare consciously kept her own countenance neutral and watched for all the body language that would help her ascertain, even more accurately, Julia's mental state. Face buried in her drawn knees, head bowed, Julia began to rock as if to propel herself to the end of her confession. "I *was* raped, because Angelica insisted I see a doctor Saturday morning." The back-and-forth movement quickened. "But only because I was terrified that I could be pregnant." Julia was now crying, and the uncontrolled sobs inhibited her ability to speak. Dr. Speare waited. "The only thing that's worse is that the really cute guy that I found dead turns out to be some pop super-star. So now I'm waiting for the police to put clues together and come question me, and then the press will get a hold of it, and when Daddy sees my picture on the front of the tabloids, he is going to *explode*. Pierce is going to know that I *cheated* on him. In less than 24 hours, my life went from perfect to a living hell."

No wonder Julia had refused to take Pierce's calls. Clearly, she was talking about Rome Ayo; Dr. Speare recalled hearing the news of his death on the rundown of the day's top stories. Thank God doctor-patient privilege clarified the ethics of what to do with Julia's information. When Julia's sobs subsided, Dr. Speare redirected Julia so that she could finish her story. "This past week, you've been at Angelica's?"

A nod. "Except when we went to Cambridge and cleaned out my room on Monday."

"What about last night?"

"I told Angelica I was going to take a bath. I broke a mirror and used the glass." Julia held up her bandaged wrists. "The rest is obvious."

After several minutes, Shae felt she could ask, "What about Pierce?"

"Pierce," Dr. Speare noted the rocking had subsided, "is literally the most perfect man. The first time I saw him—I only stopped to talk because he is really handsome. We were on a beach in Martha's Vineyard. He was polite, but he was sad, and I remember wanting to see him happy. That became my challenge. And I think growing to love me has made him happy. I know he's over ten years older than me, and at first that was kind of a big deal. But we weren't really romantically involved at first, just friends." From force of habit, Julia automatically reached for her phone, and smiled sheepishly as she realized it was not in her pocket. "I was going to show you his picture."

Shae purposely remained quiet, not yet sure how Julia would react to hearing that the man being described had sat in her same seat only a couple hours ago. Julia interpreted the silence as a cue to continue: "You know I said Daddy can be overbearing? I am positive that Pierce has never done anything without my father's permission. I've known Pierce four years, and can count on one hand the number of times he's kissed me. He's been so *patient*, waiting for me, to finish college, to grow up, to tell me he loves me. And then, look what I've done to him." Julia's rocking resumed. "I can't imagine facing him. Ever since this happened, I've avoided him. I'm sure he's worried, but I just *can't*—"Julia raised her head, her face stained with tears. "Is it okay if we stop now? I need to *do* something—stretch, move? Is that okay? Am I allowed to do that?"

Dr. Speare stood and reached out her hand to help Julia up and then held her close for a professional moment. Hugs conveyed acceptance, empathy, support. "I want you to move, Julia; in fact, exercise can be really helpful. It puts you back in control. But given what you've been through, we don't want you exert yourself, and I will have to keep you under surveillance because—"

"I know." Julia pulled away and once again held up her wrists. "I don't think I was trying to kill myself, though, Dr. Speare. I was just trying to avoid facing how one bad decision, one misadventure—caught me throwing away everything I valued in my life."

After Shae walked Julia to the exercise studio and conferred with the personal trainer who was on-staff—Julia would be limited to some easy yoga stretches and tai chi—Dr. Speare stopped at the nurses' station to pick up a chart for another patient. A folded copy of the *Times*, delivered each day for the waiting room, was beside the computer, and she noticed one of the headlines. Was it coincidence or serendipity? A few hours later, Dr. Speare explained she had an errand to run on her lunch break, drove to a nearby convenience store where she bought gas, her own copy of *The Times* and a bottle of pomegranate juice. She drank it as she read the article in the driver's seat of her Lexus.

New York City's Senior Medical Examiner released the death certificate today for pop icon Rome Ayo, who was found dead in The Vault, an exclusive New York City night club last Saturday morning. While the cause of death is hyperthermia, an autopsy also revealed Ayo's blood alcohol level at the time of death was in the .120 range. He had also taken Flunitrazepam, a prescription narcotic that can intensify intoxication and may depress respiration. "Under the influence of drugs and alcohol, Mr. Ayo most likely passed out in the hot tub, and his internal temperature rose to dangerous levels. His death was a tragic, senseless accident. No foul play was indicated."

Ty Katz, the owner of The Vault who found Ayo, confirmed his client was at the bar before Ayo checked into one of the upstairs suites. "He did not seem intoxicated at that time." However, alcohol was found near Ayo's body. He was alone when he died.

Ayo's body is being returned to his boyhood home in Verona, TN, where funeral arrangements are pending.

There was more, about Ayo's rise to stardom, and more tributes from those that either had known or admired him. Dr. Speare ripped off the front page, and folded it into her purse. Before she left for the evening, she checked on Julia, who was in her room with Sam, picking at a salad. "Not hungry?" Julia shook her head. "You have increased your water intake, though?'

"Sam's been handing me a glass of water every half hour and has watched me drink it."

"Why don't you come with me; I have something to show you."

Back in Shae's office, Julia read the article. "Does this mean I don't have to worry about the police knocking on my door and accusing me of being a killer?"

"It's not quite that simple. If you are afraid of being implicated, even though you were the original victim, you will always worry."

"I'm not sure what I should do." Another drawn-up-knees retreat into the armchair. "Angelica thinks I should press sexual assault charges."

"Have you thought about it?"

"What's the use? If Rome Ayo drugged and assaulted anyone else, they most likely can't remember to corroborate me. And he's dead, so I already know he won't be able to hurt anyone else. Because of his celebrity, though, there would be a media circus. I don't want that. They'd drag *me* through the mud. I can't let him continue to control me."

"It can be difficult to conceal the truth."

"I know." Julia handed the clipping back to Dr. Speare. "I need to think."

"Why don't you take the weekend? Call your father. It's probably safe to tell him about your anxiety attack and say that you wanted some time to process everything. You can honestly tell him that you've gone away to think things through. We'll talk again Monday morning, although you can reach me before then, if you need to."

Julia requested a notepad and some pens and wrote "What, if . . . ?" in the top margin.

On Saturday, Julia, waking early, began the dismal task of contemplating each fearful point involved in not revealing the truth. Was keeping the details of that night a secret the same as telling a lie? Would someone in the future recognize her as the last woman seen with Rome and insist on asking questions? How many questions would Daddy ask about her panic attack before he was satisfied? What was Pierce thinking, now that she had avoided him for over a week? Just because she could not remember the details of being raped, didn't mean that it hadn't happened. How as she supposed to deal with that trauma . . . with the image of a dead man in a pool of bubbling waters? Would she ever need to tell a bold-face lie, and if she did, how many lies would it beget? Were the outcomes she imagined logical? Or merely results twisted and warped by her own hideous fears?

Julia found sleep eluded her. She filled pages with stream-of-consciousness writing and then tried to bring order to it by recopying the main ideas in neat bullet points. She cried. Forty-two hours were spent in reflection. However, when they were over, Julia was certain of what she must do to redeem herself, at least when it came to Pierce.

NINETEEN

W̲HEN JULIA ARRIVED FOR HER SESSION mid-morning on Monday, Dr. Speare immediately noticed a positive change in her demeanor. She seemed more self-assured; the uncertainty had dissipated. Her bandages were also fresh, and less obtrusive than the original. "I hear you've already worked out this morning and that you ate some breakfast."

"Yes, and I've done *a lot* of thinking the past two days and wrote everything down so we could talk." Julia held up a notepad.

"Do you want me to read it?"

"I'm not sure it's legible to anyone but me." Julia glanced down at the yellow-lined pages. "Anyway, the question I really thought about is, 'What happens if I tell the truth?' I didn't even make out a page for Angelica. She already knows; she is someone I totally trust; in fact, I've realized Rome Ayo is probably better off dead than having to deal with her. She would have tortured him before she killed him, and I am not exaggerating."

"Who *did* you think about then?" asked Dr. Speare.

Julia looked down at her top page. "Ty. He knows the truth, too. And I've even thought about him someday blackmailing me, but he knows if Daddy ever found out what happened to me, he'd put that club of Ty's out of business so fast. I may feel differently if Ty ever faces any charges for negligence or something, but I can't imagine—based on what was in the paper—that he would. It's not like he was liable; Rome got that drunk and high on—whatever—when he was in his own room. And I'm sure that guests use those rooms at their own risk. But if Ty *would* be sued and *if* his lawyers can't make the case go away, I won't let my cousin perjure himself."

Julia sighed and flipped the pages. "My parents—fairly easy. I've heard Mother talk about her dead children at her Foundation's benefits for years, and I don't want her to think that I almost did something that could have added me to her list. Daddy would be so furious, I know he would do something to Ty and cause even more trouble between Mother and her sister." Julia lay the notepad down on the coffee table in front of her chair.

"So," summarized Dr. Speare, "I'm hearing you say there's really no need to tell anyone what you've shared with me?"

"I haven't told you yet about the pages I wrote out for Pierce."

Julia's voice quivered. "I think when it comes to Pierce, he *does* need to know. And I'm expecting him to be shocked and hurt. But I will guarantee him one thing: I will *never* do anything like that again. Somehow, I need to convince him that the whole Rome Ayo in The Vault experience was a complete fluke." The tears had started trailing down Julia's cheeks and she paused to wipe them away. "What will be the hardest is letting *him* decide if he still can love me." Julia looked directly at Shae. "Where I need your help, Dr. Speare, is figuring out the words to say to him. And if he can't deal with what I tell him, I really will need therapy."

"Well, then." Dr. Speare clicked her pen and snagged a piece of paper from her own desk. "Let's get started. And once you know what you want to say to Pierce, we can talk about possible outcomes so you won't feel blindsided, no matter what Pierce decides."

TWENTY

Two days later

PIERCE PULLED THE KEYS FROM THE ignition and sat for several seconds in the parking lot of Global Health. It had been not quite six days since he had left. During that time, he had thrown himself once again into his work, his way to avoid the heavy burden of feelings. Loren Cappell's showing up unexpected and unannounced at his office late Friday, when Pierce was still sinking beneath the oppressive events of the previous night, had been the worst part of his inauspicious week. "Did you know about Julia's panic attack?" Loren had demanded.

Cappell was one of those rare souls who had never experienced a nanosecond of self-doubt, who harbored absolutely no insecurities. Pierce had feigned nonchalance over a mere panic attack—*Was that the Julia's euphemism for slashing her wrists with broken glass?*—though he agreed that Julia did *not* seem to be the type to succumb to anxiety. "But," Pierce had continued casually, "I've heard anxiety is quite common in periods of transition." He'd also lied: "Julia mentioned the night of graduation that she was a little worried about her future. I suggested she go off by herself for a few days if she needed to so that she could map out her life. After all, Sir, when I ask her to marry me, I want her to say 'yes' because she feels confident that that's what she really wants. I don't want her to say 'yes' because she feels pressured to do what's expected." Pierce had even apologized that Loren had not known: "I assumed, Sir, she told you first that she was going away." But when Pierce heard himself expressing utmost confidence that, "Of course,

Julia will start her job at Cappell Properties the beginning of July, just like you two agreed"—he had wondered how he could sound so sure.

On Saturday, Angelica called him, thrilled. She had just gotten off the phone with Julia. (A visceral blow that Julia had yet to contact him.) "Pierce," Angela paused as their brief conversation drew to a close. "Julia asked me how she got from my apartment to the hospital to that clinic where she's at. I *had* to tell her how I called you to help me, and I could tell it really upset her. She's just, I guess, embarrassed, you know? She's never wanted to make people go to any trouble. My God, when she was little, she would apologize for puking when she had the flu! But any way, if it weren't for you . . . I am so grateful you came. I suck at crisis situations."

Finally, yesterday afternoon, Dr. Speare had contacted Pierce, asking if he would be able to come to Global on Wednesday evening. And now it was almost 8:00 P.M. on Wednesday. Although it was still light and quite warm, Pierce felt cold. He could almost hear the blood pounding in his veins as he stepped from the car. *Would she confess the cause of her strange behavior?* Julia, if she had a dark side, was not cunning enough to hide it. What event had scared her into attempting to take her life? *And did she love him?* He did not yet know if she would say yes. Perhaps the gods would laugh and prove Diane's prophecy mere perjury. Still, his trust that Diane's farewell words were true made Pierce return to pull the jeweler's case from the glove box, remove his grandmother's diamond, and place it in his pocket.

Dr. Speare herself greeted Pierce. She explained, when he expressed surprise, that she worked late one night each week to better serve the patients' families. She escorted him to the back, where Julia, no longer pale, was already waiting in the landscaped courtyard, perched on a wicker sofa. The bandages around her wrists were hardly visible because of the way she had crossed her hands. "You should know," said Dr. Speare before Pierce pushed the door open, "that this area, like everyplace else in this facility, is monitored by cameras. So, if you run into any trouble—if Julia were to become agitated or hysterical—someone will be right out. But I am incredibly confident that everything will be fine—if you just let her do the talking. Think monologue, not dialogue, at least for a while."

Pierce squared his shoulders as he headed toward her. No need to postpone what was to be. "Hello." He was careful to smile when Julia looked up, and he asked permission to sit beside her. He lowered himself to the floral cushion, caught the scent of her perfume, and rested his elbow against the back of his seat so that he could face her at an angle, although she looked straight ahead once she finally started to speak. As he listened, Pierce found himself searching for a word to describe Julia's tone of voice. Not exactly fear or sorrow. Her words were wrapped in regret and presented to him with apprehension. Strung together, they were an admission ("I've spend most of my time here trying to work up the courage to tell you some ugly facts"), and a plea ("Please, please, just hear me out.") For a brief second, he recalled Diane's revelation and how much Julia's account of her recent past was likewise a mere summary of the essentials. Julia described the symptoms of the panic attack that had so disconcerted her father; a psychiatrist's advice to do something 'out of character;' her arranging a trip to her cousin Ty's club; her next and only memory: an attentive celebrity-type who, it turned out, spiked her drink; then waking up in a strange room, blood on the sheets.

Pierce's imagination conjured the details she omitted. He visualized Julia walking into The Vault. The blaring music and flashing lights. A leering lothario immediately deducing Julia's innocence and slipping something into her drink. Whoever he was, Pierce hated him. Even though Julia did not use the word "rape," Pierce knew she had been the victim of that vile act. *Thank God she does not remember it.*

Weeping, almost silently, Julia seemed to have finished her confession. With his thumb, Pierce reached over to wipe away the tears trickling from the corners of her eyes. She held his hand against her cheek as she continued. "There's something else. I know you always keep up with the news. You heard about the singer that died?" Pierce did remember seeing the articles, but had only skimmed them. Another pop idol whose own vices had led to his death, in Pierce's mind, was not bona fide news, until Julia whispered, "He was . . . the one. In fact, I found him."

A phrase in print became a vivid mental image; *was alone when he died.* Julia anticipated Pierce's question before he could ask. "Ty took charge almost right away, and so far, no one seems to doubt his version of events. I didn't talk to anyone other than Rome at The Vault, and Ty told me that celebrities usually don't notice other people unless they are more famous than they are. Still . . . What if someone *does* remember seeing me? *That* was why I . . . that night Ang found me—she told me she called you so Daddy wouldn't find out. Pierce, I am *so* sorry that you had to see me like that, so *sorry* that

I even did it. I was desperate, though, to forget. To make my guilty deed go away . . . I beg you, please forgive me. I will never do anything like that again."

Julia did not resist when Pierce, pulling her back against him, almost instinctively wrapped his arms around her to assure her she was forgiven. What had she really done wrong anyway? Her vulnerability pressed against him, trembling. "You're scared, aren't you?" He kissed her temple softly, rhythmically in lieu of words. Of all the young women he had ever encountered, Julia was the one who was least prepared to deal with the situation in which she had found herself. Loren Cappell and Angelica's protectiveness, Julia's own sweet, trusting, compliant nature had set her up to truly be a victim, and Pierce knew he would be wrong to blame or berate her. "So, all this is why you didn't take my calls, why you shut me out?" Pierce could feel her nod beneath his chin. "When you panicked, you could have told me. I would have given you space."

"But space wasn't what I needed." The twilight had intensified, and the growing darkness seemed to increase Julia's confidence, for her words came more easily, were less rehearsed. "What started all this, was that awful Dr. Lawrence telling me that my life was too much like a script. And even though I agreed at first, I know now that the script isn't the problem. The script is wonderful. The issue is that, I didn't know if I deserved to keep playing it. Maybe the part was written for Elinor or Vincent. I mean, what college graduate with no experience is offered a corner office and a starting salary of a quarter million dollars?"

Perhaps Julia intended her question to be rhetorical, but Pierce still answered, "The daughter of the great Loren "Rich" Cappell; surely you expected him to hire you after last summer. And you should be flattered. Your father trusts you with the business that has been his life."

"All right," Julia conceded. "But then . . . why am I worthy of you? What about *me* has made you willing to jump through every hoop of my father's and wait *four* years to tell me you love me? What will happen if I can't pull the next act off? What if you find out . . . that I wasn't worth the time or the trouble?"

Julia twisted in his embrace and her arms crept around his neck. She laid her head on his shoulder, her tears dampening the fabric of his shirt. How to reassure her? The curse of Julia's being blessed with beauty and fortune was her fear that people only loved her for those superficial qualities and that she could never disappoint them by being less than perfect.

Pierce pulled away, just enough so that he could look into her still glistening eyes. Her return gaze did not falter. "Julia Paige Cappell." He used her full name, for this was an official declaration: "I love you. And that means, even when I find out you aren't perfect, I must always believe with all my heart that you are still perfect for me."

She seemed to wait, but Pierce had no more to say. Surely she already knew he would lay his own fortune at her feet to follow her anywhere in the world. Slowly, Julia leaned forward and kissed him. "Someday, Conrad Pierce, when you are absolutely sure you can trust me again, will you please marry me?"

For a moment, Pierce wondered if she had uttered the words he'd heard, or if he were only dreaming, but the lightness that had replaced his heavy heart was too compelling to doubt: "I am sure. Right now."

A kiss to seal the bargain. ("Wow!" murmured Brooke, who was monitoring the courtyard camera inside at the nurses' station with more interest than usual.) And then Pierce slipped his grandmother's ring on Julia's finger, where it sparkled like little stars cut from the night sky (and elicited from Brooke the pronouncement, "Now *that* is a rock!")

The next morning, when Julia showed her engagement ring to Dr. Shaelyn Speare, the diamond shone even brighter in the sun. Their session focused that morning on the benchmarks Julia would have to meet to demonstrate she was ready and able to leave Global Health—maybe by the end of the week.

TWENTY ONE

One month later

Ty Katz was finally starting to breathe easier. The first couple days after the whole Rome Ayo debacle had been rough. After returning from dropping off Julia, he had been careful to clean Rome's room thoroughly enough to ensure that any trace of Julia's presence would be eliminated, but not so thoroughly that detectives dusting for prints would think he had been trying to cover something up. Clearly, if detectives knew about Julia, then Ty had motive; as the owner of the club, he had opportunity, too; and someone might construe the alcohol and hot tub as Ty's means to kill Rome. *Thank God he had never mentioned to anyone that Julia was his cousin or even Cappell's daughter.* He had merely told the driver who picked her up at the airport that some rich kid wanted to party. Preserving anonymity was second nature to him by now. He was glad he hadn't had time to pull Julia into his office to sign the standard contract, either. Rome had moved in too fast, which fortunately meant hardly anyone had seen her.

So the suite had been cleaned, and the sheets were in the wash for the second time before Ty had called the police—911 so that it would seem like he had just encountered the body. Julia assured him she had never gone near the hot tub, so Ty hadn't really cleaned in there, and was almost pleased to see the fifth of Gentleman Jack almost empty and within arm's-reach of the tub. Booze and a hot tub; it wouldn't take a rocket scientist to connect the dots. The one detective had been a bit of a prick, though. Why was the *owner* of a hugely successful nightclub for the rich and famous doing the cleaning himself? "Because my service is discretion, and I can't risk a cleaning lady leaking some juicy bit of gossip to the tabloids." You could pay her enough to make a bribe less tempting. "I'll be damned if I pay her half a million a year to pull sheets off the bed and mop floors." Why no surveillance? "Private property, and remember, my service is utmost discretion. Besides, no camera can monitor like me and my staff." Mr. Katz seemed to work awfully hard for someone who was so successful. "Newsflash. I'm successful because I work hard." Hadn't Mr. Katz thought it might be a good idea to check on Mr. Ayo? "I didn't realize hotel managers make it standard procedure to go into guests' rooms to check on them." So the suites were like a standard hotel's? "In some ways. Guests check in, and are supposed to be out by noon. When I didn't see a 'Do not disturb' sign, I knocked and went into Ayo's room to get a head start on cleaning. Saturday nights, the suites are always in demand." When had Mr. Ayo gone up to his room? "Pretty early. Well before 11:00, but he had complained about being exhausted after a string of concerts and promotional appearances."

After talking to the detective, Ty had written everything he said down and read and re-read it until he almost believed that this version was what had really transpired. He also pulled Rome's agreement and called his lawyer— just in case. When the coroner's report was released, Ty breathed a sigh of relief. The fact that the ruffies were in Rome's system too had been a bonus. He tried calling Julia to see if she had gone in for a rape kit, but there was no answer, and he left no message.

Now, it was mid-July; the celebrity news cycle had moved on, and Ty was heading north on I-87 in order to check out the Empire City Casino. He knew he couldn't obtain a gambling license for The Vault, but he wanted to install a video game station that would simulate casino gaming, and needed to investigate how he could best recreate the casino experience. It was a sunny afternoon, so he took the club's only convertible and put the top down. A little before 2:00, his cell vibrated with an incoming call. "Hello?"

"Hey, Katz! How you doing? This is Murray Q."

What kind of man uses only an initial as his last name? "What can I do for you, Murray?"

"*Rolling Stone* is trying to put together some sort of retrospective for Rome Ayo. Since The Vault was the last place Rome was seen alive, I'd like to talk to you."

Ty laughed, because that's what he would normally do if some reporter asked to interview him, and Ty found it was still taking deliberate effort to seem normal. "You want to book my place so that you can hold some sort of a memorial wake there? I like it. I think Rome would have, too."

"Actually, I just wanted to see what you can remember about Rome that night."

Along with never divulging names, Ty's other rule was to count to ten when anyone asked him a question about a client. Since anything having to do with Rome was now more complicated, he counted to fifteen. On the other end, he heard Murray Q. ask if he was still there. "Yeah, I am." Fifteen seconds, and his response was perfect. "Hey, I totally understand what you're trying to do, and, you know, I liked Rome a lot; it was always great to see him walk into the club. But if I talk about him on camera or for your magazine, then my other clients are going to wonder if I'll talk about them someday, too. I don't want to seem crass or anything, but they're the ones who are still paying to come to The Vault, not Rome. Besides, everything I know, I've already told the police. Sorry I can't think of anything else. Trust me, I've tried."

Ty let Murray end the call, but was so engrossed in wondering whether his answer had disarmed the reporter that he failed to check his mirrors when he pulled into the passing lane. *Why are out-of-state drivers always so freaking slow?*

The Escalade Ty broadsided, traveling at 80 mph, flipped Ty's BMW 4 Series, which then skidded into another lane of traffic, right into a semi's path.

State troopers pronounced Ty Katz dead at the scene.

TWENTY TWO

Labor Day Weekend

JULIA AND PIERCE DECIDED TO BE married in December in St. Mortiz—a small ceremony where the only guests would be immediate family. Even though Ty had been estranged from her family for years, Julia, in particular, said she would prefer that to having an elaborate wedding when her aunt was still in mourning. "Then I won't invite her to your engagement party," Loren Cappell countered. "After all, it's been planned for a year since I had to book the Harbor View in advance."

Loren Cappell loved to host parties. For years, he had invited key associates and friends to an end of summer gala on Martha's Vineyard. When he served as U.S. Senator, the festivities had assumed a political air, attended by big campaign donors and other movers and shakers in the party and national politics. One year, the President had even been in attendance. This year, it had morphed into an engagement celebration, with the addition of some of Pierce's family and, of course, the closest friends of the couple. A perfect location, given that Martha's Vineyard was where Pierce and Julia had first met.

Patricia, in a sudden burst of maternal sentiment, had joined Angelica while the stylist arranged Julia's hair (Pierce preferred she wear it down) and applied her makeup. Back in June, Angelica had accompanied Julia to the dressmaker's to design her outfit for tonight. Julia had extracted from her purse two matching cuff bracelets, an early birthday gift from Pierce, selected because they were wide enough to hide the still-visible scars on her wrists with diamonds on thin intersecting strands of gold. "I'd like something that will set these off." They had both approved the designer's creation: a cream, off-the shoulder sheath, fitted to emphasize Julia' small waist, tapered to the bottom of her knee with a kick pleat in the back. "I'll have to take baby steps," observed Julia as she stood in front of the mirror during the final fitting, trying on different shoes. (They finally selected gold stiletto sandals.)

"Sweetie, the whole point of that dress is to make everyone realize how lucky Pierce is. Whether you walk or not is immaterial."

Now that Julia was dressed and would not appear until Loren introduced Pierce after the dinner, Angelica sat in the lobby of the Harbor View, where many of the guests were staying, gratis of course. (No one could ever say that Loren was cheap.) A string quartet played in the corner, protégés of Pierce's mother. His sisters, Catherine and Candace, arrived early, and knew her well enough that each gave her a hug. Josie and Brianna—giddy with excitement in their fancy dresses and "princess slippers"—made Angelica wistful for the days when Julia was their age. *Crap, she was going to cry.* She fished for a tissue in her purse. Hopefully, Julia and Pierce would soon have pretty babies for her to take care of, even though Julia had confided that Pierce wanted to wait to have children so that she could focus on her career first. One of Julia's Harvard housemates recognized her, and Angelica pretended to listen as she rattled off her plans for graduate school. As the cocktail hour that would precede the dinner began, faces familiar from the Foundation's benefits and from parties in years past drifted by. The guests kissed or shook hands with Loren, who had been paired with Celia to greet them, and then repeated the kisses with Patricia, and the handshakes with Hank. But, Angelica thought, not a single guest could claim to know Julia like she did. She had raised the Cappells' daughter whom they had all come to see. JuJu Bean was hers, her Sweetie—if only until December.

The engraved invitations stated that dinner would be served at 7:30, and Angelica delayed entering the dining room until 25 minutes after. Already impressive with its columns and chandelier suspended from the elevated skylight, the dining room was even more beautiful with lavish rose bouquets on each table and place settings of silver and crystal arranged on snowy white linen. Waiters circulated with champagne cocktails and hors d'oeuvres. Behind a glass wall, Angelica noted the many guests who preferred hard liquor had gathered at the bar. She herself decided she could use a gin fizz.

Soon after, the Cappells and Pierces were seated, and the waiters began dealing out salads. A small design beside each guests' name card indicated whether they were to be served filet mignon, chicken cordon bleu or glazed salmon once their salad plates were whisked away. Angelica had been seated at a table of Julia's college friends, most of whom came without escorts. "I just can't see myself getting married yet!" one of them almost squealed. (No wonder. She was still a girl, and Julia was a woman.) Another, who would be starting medical school in a week lamented, "I'm not even going to have *time* to date for the next four years." (But she didn't have a man like Pierce waiting in the wings either, did she?) "Do you remember the flowers he'd send her every day?" added the girl sitting to Angelica's right. "I mean, that was so romantic."

Angelica wanted to tell them it was more than romance. What other red-blooded young man would have waited as long as Pierce had? And the fact that he, without a trace of anger or blame, had managed the fallout of Julia's lapse in judgment this past June proved to Angelica once and for all that she could trust Pierce with her Julia. Not to mention how, when Ty was killed in that awful car accident, it was Pierce who had helped a still-fragile Julia from once again disintegrating, who had convinced her that Ty's death was *not* her fault. Pierce alone had supported her, both literally and emotionally, throughout the day of Ty's very private funeral. That willingness to stand by Julia's side so she could lean on him was proof of Pierce's love. Romance seemed paltry in comparison.

As the plates from the entrée were being cleared, Loren rose from his place at the head table. Oh yes, he loved to hear himself speak, to be the center of attention, and so he amplified his already resonant baritone with a microphone so that the entire room immediately hushed. "Once again, I would like to thank everyone for coming this evening. Of all the treasures I have accumulated throughout my life and career, I count those of you in this room to be the greatest."

For someone who could be so abrasive, Loren Cappell could dole out sap, too, and at these parties, he tended to be downright schmaltzy. Angelica turned on her camera, ready to take pictures as Loren continued, "Some of you have been friends for many years. Some of you are sitting here for the first time, and that is because you have all come to help celebrate the fact that I am honored, yes, honored to introduce to you a young man I respect and admire for his integrity, his intelligence, and above all, his devotion to my daughter. Ladies and gentlemen, please join me in welcoming the man I will soon call my son-in-law: Mr. Conrad Pierce!"

Angelica felt her heart swell and joined in the applause. The string quartet had played throughout dinner. But now the music, upbeat Broadway, wafted from the sound system as Pierce appeared in the doorway, holding Julia's hand. Angelica clapped until her hands hurt; they were so incredibly beautiful together. Pierce raised their joined arms above their heads, and with the other, made a sweeping gesture to indicate the room should continue their applause for his future bride, and then, through a standing ovation, he led Julia to Loren, who relinquished the microphone. "Thank you." Pierce had to repeat himself three times before the applause died down. "I am very humbled by your welcome, humbled by the fact that the woman standing beside me, who is brilliant in so many ways, has agreed to marry me. Hopefully, Julia and I will be able to personally thank each and every one of you for coming. We'll start making the rounds while you enjoy dessert."

Fourteen tables, most seating eight people, were arranged around the room. Still holding hands, as if they were extensions of each other, Pierce and Julia began to circulate among them, and those who sat at the tables yet to be greeted lingered there, drinking coffee, ordering more drinks, unwilling to relinquish the opportunity to mingle with the mesmerizing young couple. Angelica's table was saved for last, and Angelica stood so that Julia could hug her more easily. "I love you, Ang." *Lord, did that make her cry.* And then Pierce hugged her, too, and thanked her for everything. *She hoped she didn't smear any makeup on his lapel.*

Only after Pierce and Julia had visited each table did the dancing begin. Celia had requested that they begin with her parents' song—the rock on Julia's finger had belonged to them, so Celia had every right to dictate the music. Another of her scholarship recipients, a silky tenor, sang as 124 guests gathered to watch Pierce and Julia's exude their special chemistry on the dance floor.

> *Time after time, I tell myself that I'm*
> *So lucky to be loving you.*
> *So lucky to be the one you run to see*
> *In the evening, when the day is through.*

I only know what I know, the passing years will show
You've kept my love so young, so new.
And time after time, you'll hear me say that I'm
So lucky to be loving you.

Pierce knew how to lead, and Julia knew how to follow effortlessly. Of course, they switched partners for the next song; Hank was not as skilled as his son, and Patricia—okay, she *was* a little uptight—was too formal to match her daughter's fluid form. Still, the symbolism of the gesture was not lost on Angelica, or anyone else: Julia and Pierce would soon join themselves to another family. A transition to both sets of parents pairing up with their spouses, and Pierce and Julia were partners again as many of the guests joined in. Angelica's eyes followed Julia. Her dream for Julia was about to come true. Julia would soon marry; her husband, an escapee from the island for perfect men—a lovely gentleman.

TWENTY-THREE

T HE OLDER GUESTS RETIRED FIRST, MANY a little after midnight, soon after Loren arranged for the hotel's wait staff to prepare a buffet table of more desserts, or, for those who preferred, chilled shrimp cocktail and *foie grass*. Pierce and Julia's friends stayed the latest, and around 1:30 in the morning, some of the more high-spirited even decided to embark on a moonlit pilgrimage to the lighthouse, visible from the back veranda of the hotel. Pierce and Julia declined, and since Loren was still in host mode, Pierce offered to drive Julia and Patricia home.

Julia was tired, but not sleepy, and it seemed only natural, after she and Pierce said good-night to her mother, that they would stroll along the beach to where she had first encountered him sleeping in the summer sun. All evening Julia had found herself indulging in one of her favorite private pastimes: looking at Pierce. So often, his chiseled good looks were eclipsed by his unfailing ability to respond to her as she desired. In fact, when Julia thought of Pierce, what always came to her mind first was the reassuring way he had pressed her hand the night of his first Foundation benefit, as if he understood what she was thinking, feeling—intuitively knowing she needed someone to make *her* feel important. More recently, thoughts of Pierce conjured a sensation of tenderness because of the way he had held her when she had confessed to him about Rome; and there was strength in Pierce, too, which she was able to draw upon, clutching his arm as he stood beside her at Ty's interment. Julia's sense of Pierce was formed primarily by tactile images, not visual. But then she would look at him and realize how handsome he truly was. Even without kissing her, Pierce could take her breath away.

Rome had done that, too, but only for a moment. The only solid recollection Julia had of that night was walking into The Vault, suddenly aware that she was making the stupidest choice of her life, uncertain as to what to do. Joining the cluster of those dancing had seemed the best way to fit in, to be unobtrusive until Rome had somehow singled her out. Being targeted by someone rightfully acknowledged for being the Sexiest Man Alive was . . . gratifying. But what was Rome? A player with sex appeal, marking out another conquest before moving on. All flattery, nothing substantial since even the words Rome had spoken to her sounded like the lyrics to one of his songs. They were not genuine but generic enough to fit any female Rome seduced. Rome may have called her an angel. But Pierce—even when he was just listening to her share details about the contracts on her desk at Cappell Properties—could communicate how much he actually cared about her. Only Pierce asked her opinion on everything from world events to the color of leather he should order for the interior of his new car since he was replacing his Jag convertible, even without her asking him to do so. He had even assured her that if she eventually decided to bring charges against Rome, he would support her. Pierce had placed her in the center of his world and had spent years proving he was willing to make everything else revolve around *her*. Rome had only wanted to add her to his collection and after a matter of minutes, had drugged her so that *he* could be satisfied.

Julia had spoken to Dr. Speare twice since leaving Global, once after Ty died. That had been a panicked call, an intense discussion about cause-and-effect versus coincidental sequence. Julia had been nowhere near the highway. Ty had made the choice to speed in a convertible, and Julia was not responsible for the choices of others. Julia called again after she and Pierce had decided on a St. Moritz wedding and honeymoon. Was it possible that, at some point in the future, Julia would suddenly remember that night with Rome—a post-traumatic flashback set off by something that might trigger repressed memories? Dr. Speare had assured Julia that because her amnesia was drug-induced, not a psychological defense mechanism, what had transpired before she woke up in Rome's suite at The Vault would forever remain a mystery. "You know *what* happened; forensic evidence proved it. But the how—those details never registered." And that had comforted Julia marvelous much, because she never wanted any touch or contact with Pierce to be marred by that one evening when her judgment had lapsed so unluckily.

Tonight, the moon was casting its silver light on the water. The sand, no longer radiating the sun's light, had lost its heat, but Pierce's arm around her was warm; her own hand cupped his solid waistline. They were approaching the place where she had first seen him, where they had first danced. Although she had found out so much about Pierce—incidental stories of his boyhood, the rise and fall of his baseball career, his time at Harvard and special memories of his grandfather—Julia was once again aware that she did not know everything about her fiancé, and that at some level, he would always be, to her, a closed book, simply because she was unaware that certain pages even existed. Perhaps there were notes in the margins of some chapters he never intended for her to read.

Still, Julia wanted to know: why her? How was it that a young man with family money, a promising future, impeccable taste and old-world manners, a model-worthy physique and face—why was he *not* already taken? Why, with his experience and sophistication, had Conrad Pierce apparently decided that a recent high-school graduate should someday become his wife? Once, she had even tried to figure out if Daddy could somehow be behind it, arranging their relationship by purchasing the summer home next to Pierce's. But even Daddy could not purchase or negotiate feelings. Catherine once alluded to a woman who had broken Pierce's heart, which would explain the sadness that had so marked Julia's first impression of him. Perhaps, Julia wondered, she should feel jealous. But why? Whoever that woman was, she had left Pierce for Julia, and by breaking his heart had refined him, fashioned Pierce into a better man capable of readily forgiving Julia when she perhaps did not deserve it, a man patient enough to be the consummate suitor.

The moonlight was now twinkling in the diamonds on her bracelets, which throughout the party had concealed the scars on each of her wrists. Suddenly, unexpectedly, the sheer terror of that night in Angelica's bathroom returned, and Julia shivered involuntarily. So ill-equipped to handle a confusing and overwhelming situation, she had impulsively attempted to end her life. And if she had, she would be dead, lying in a tomb, not be here, right now, full of life with Pierce. Standing in the starlight, the tide ebbing at their bare feet, Julia experienced an epiphany: loving Pierce meant that Julia would never look for a way to die for him. She would choose to live, to celebrate each day they shared, to grow old with him, and someday, one would continue to live on, if only to remember they may not have been perfect, but that they had found a way to be truly perfect for each other.

"Oh happy dagger
Here is thy sheath; there rust and let me die"?
A tragic ending, indeed.

Beth Fuchs

Study Guide for *The Properer Man*

1. One of the most obvious similarities between Shakespeare's play *Romeo and Juliet* and the novella *The Properer Man* are the characters. Identify the characters who match up with the *dramatis personae* listed below:

   Sampson
   Gregory
   Benvolio
   Tybalt, "Prince of Cats"
   Romeo
   Count Paris
   Lord Capulet
   Lady Capulet
   The Nurse
   Juliet Capulet
   Mercutio
   Friar Laurence

2. Focus on the characters of Loren and Patricia Cappell, Julia Cappell, Conrad Pierce, Angelica Nurre, and Ty Katz. How do they resemble the Shakespeare characters who inspired them? Consider their personalities as well as other details, like age and socio-economic class.

3. In Arthur Brooke's poem, which inspired Shakespeare's *Romeo and Juliet*, Mercutio is simply a guest at the Capulet party. Shakespeare transformed that part into a fairly major role. Likewise, the importance of characters in *The Properer Man* varies from the Shakespeare play. Which characters' roles are diminished? Which are expanded? How does this affect the plot?

4. Although Shakespeare mentions the goddess Diane to clarify the demeanor of his play's never-seen character of Rosaline—Romeo's initial crush—Diane becomes a major character in *The Properer Man*. What purpose does she serve?

5. Explain how the psychiatrist's name is both a pun and allusion.

6. Shakespeare wrote plays to be performed at the Globe Theater during the reign of King James I; how is this information reflected in the text?

7. Below are passages in the novella that are allusions to Shakespeare's play *Romeo and Juliet*. Identify their Shakespearean counterparts and identify them by act, scene, and line number:

Chapter One

 a. *Best Album Grammy Award last year for* Cold Fire
 b. *The Vault, an exclusive New York City night spot that caters to celebrities*
 c. *Ayo was born in Verona, TN*
 d. *His first top forty song, "Rosaline"*
 e. *Whose album* I Am Too Bold *sold over 10 million copies*
 f. *Rome Ayo can never again be dismissed as a pretty face that should front a boy-band. He has proven he is, in every sense, a man who is a legitimate contender in the field."*

Chapter Two

 a. The gray pre-dawn sky was flecked with streaks of light

Chapter Three

 a. overwhelmed by inundation of tears

Chapter Four

 a. sail-to-the-farthest-shores infatuated with her

Chapter Five

 a. He asked the waiter for a box and that evening ate her sesame chicken for his supper, remembering how he loved her company.

Chapter Seven

a. I've denied my father and refused to use his name, but I still want to take care of my mom and Debbie and give Troy real options."

b. Diane Garret drifted beyond his reach, out of his life, leaving him still beguiled, but now spited and spurned.

Chapter Nine

a. He slipped into a daydream where she called to express her condolences, where one thing led to another—a vain fantasy born of his sorrow.

Chapter Ten

a. ". . . I'll find out and see that you are whipped, tormented and deprived of your food."

Chapter Eleven

a. He liked the way Julia shone in light blue velvet, surrounded by all the black tuxedos, a rich jewel in the night, much like the diamond earrings dangling against her smooth cheeks.

b. "The earth swallowed four of our children, but my hope is that their deaths have not been in vain.

c. and a faint blush painted her cheeks when she saw that he was speaking the truth.

d. "He said roses are only for lovers, and that lilies smelled just as sweet."

Chapter Twelve

a. Pierce only wished that July 31st, Julia's twenty-second birthday, were tomorrow.

Chapter Thirteen

a. "You should most definitely write a book about your technique."

b. He hoped Cappell would agree to a short engagement, and then it would be only a year until he could call her "Mine."

c. Pierce's sense of anticipation overwhelmed him as the winter limped into spring. There was the sensual delight of being in Julia's presence when she surprised him on his birthday in April, just as he was leaving the office. (Her gift: a studio portrait of herself, only head and shoulders visible, taken from above, so that she was looking up as if she were emerging from a bouquet of roses.)

d. (Sometimes Pierce had felt like Julia's father wanted his daughter to be on a tether that he could pull back, so unwilling was he to give her any liberty.)

Chapter Fourteen

a. "And she takes me back to this bedroom where there was the prettiest baby. She was able to stand, but wasn't real steady yet, and she went down—BAM! —and started to cry. I just picked her up and fell in love. Later, I found out that she and my Susan were born not even a day apart.

Chapter Fifteen

a. But once they grow up, Sweetie, not all men are liars

b. I will make your daddy look like a worn-out dishcloth."

c. (Her periodontist at one point declared she was at risk of having only four teeth left.)

d. But it was his interactions with Julia that held Angelica's attention the most. Something about them reminded Angelica of how she had felt one time when Nana Susan had bought her this to-die-for white dress with flowers embroidered on it, and a full skirt that flared out when she twirled. Angelica had wanted to wear it right then, but Nana said she must wait until her cousin's wedding. Angelica realized Pierce, no matter how crazy he was about Julia, had clearly been told he must wait until the wedding, too.

e. "You'll finish college next year, Sweetie, and something tells me your graduation present from him is going to be a big, beautiful diamond. I'll bet every last one of my teeth on it."

f. Pierce, by waiting, had proven his was a gentleman-like offer

Chapter Sixteen

a. Perhaps Pierce had finally . . . God forgive her for actually hoping.

Chapter Seventeen

a. Cold fear thrills that Rome Ayo's lawyers might be better than his

b. Silently, Ty cursed her womanish tears.

c. Thank God it was still so early; the birds were still singing to herald the morning.

Chapter Eighteen

a. Seated in a deep arm chair, her long dark hair still wet, Julia looked almost like a child or a stranger in an alien world.

b. I was just trying to avoid facing how one bad decision, one misadventure—caught me throwing away everything I valued in my life."

Chapter Nineteen

a. Julia, waking early, began the dismal task of contemplating each fearful point involved in not revealing the truth.

b. Were the outcomes she imagined logical? Or merely results twisted and warped by her own hideous fears?

c. Forty-two hours were spent in reflection

Chapter Twenty

a. Pierce was still sinking beneath the oppressive events of the previous night

b. had been the worst part of his inauspicious week.

c. *Would she confess the cause of her strange behavior? And did she love him?* He did not yet know if she would say yes. Perhaps the gods would laugh and prove Diane's prophecy mere perjury.
d. Pierce knew he would be wrong to blame or berate her.
e. The daughter of the great rich Loren Cappell; surely you expected him to hire you after last summer
f. Surely she already knew he would lay his own fortune at her feet to follow her anywhere in the world.
g. Pierce wondered if she had uttered the words he'd heard, or if he were only dreaming, but the lightness that had replaced his heavy heart was too compelling to doubt
h. A kiss to seal the bargain
i. then Pierce slipped his grandmother's ring on Julia's finger, where it sparkled like little stars cut from the night sky

Chapter Twenty Two

a. Her dream for Julia was about to come true. Julia would soon marry; her husband, an escapee from the island for perfect men—a lovely gentleman.

Chapter Twenty-Three

a. a little after midnight, soon after Loren arranged for the hotel's wait staff to prepare a buffet table of more desserts, or, for those who preferred, chilled shrimp cocktail and *foie grass*
b. All flattery, nothing substantial since even the words Rome had spoken to her sounded like the lyrics to one of his songs.
c. Rome may have called her an angel.
d. And that had comforted Julia marvelous much, because she never wanted any touch or contact with Pierce to be marred by that one evening when her judgment had lapsed so unluckily.
e. Pierce would always be, to her, a closed book, simply because she was unaware that certain pages even existed. Perhaps there were notes in the margins of some chapters he never intended for her to read.

ANSWER KEY

1.

Sampson	Samantha, the nurse
Gregory	Gracy, the nurse
Benvolio	Ben Volaire, Rome Ayo's agent
Tybalt, "Prince of Cats"	Ty Katz, Julia's cousin
Romeo	Rome Ayo
Count Paris	Conrad Pierce
Lord Capulet	Loren Cappell
Lady Capulet	Patricia Cappell
The Nurse	Angelica Nurre
Juliet Capulet	Julia Cappell
Mercutio	Murray Q., critic for *Rolling Stone*
Friar Laurence	Dr. Laurence

2. **Loren Cappell**, like Lord Capulet, is very wealthy, insistent on his own way, controlling of his daughter, a good host. **Patricia Cappell,** like Lady Capulet, is not involved in the day-to-day raising of her daughter; she has lost several children, too. She impresses others as uptight, and she may not be happily married. **Julia**, like Juliet, is young, beautiful, obedient, naïve and therefore vulnerable, anxious to please. They share the same birthday. **Pierce**, like Paris, is mature, polite, diplomatic, willing to make a commitment, handsome and well-built, from a wealthy family, and devoted to the idea of marrying a lovely female younger than he is. He even has green eyes. **Angelica**, like the Nurse, is from a lower-class background; she has lost a daughter named Susan; her conversation is more crude and "earthy" than that of the other characters. She adores Juliet and possesses her confidence, which she never loses (although in the original, her advice to marry Paris causes a rift in her relationship with her young charge). Also, in Act Four, it seems that Capulet calls the Nurse by name "Angelica" when he asks her to look after the meats. Hence her name in *The Properer Man* is Angelica. **Ty Katz,** like Tybalt, is

the Cappells' nephew who does **not** always say yes to his dominating uncle. Tybalt's ability and willingness to fight is unneeded, however, since the feud has been eliminated as a central conflict. Like Tybalt, Ty dies unexpectedly.

3. Paris (Pierce) becomes the protagonist, to emphasize the fact that he would have been the better choice for Juliet (Julia). All Pierce's relatives were invented for this novella. The Capulets (Cappells) all have a role approximate with their role in the original play as does the Nurse (Angelica) and Tybalt (Ty Katz). The most diminished role is that of Friar Laurence (Dr. Laurence), whose advice is to Juliet/Julia is highly questionable in both pieces. The role of Romeo (Rome Ayo) is also reduced to his obituary and mere descriptions, another reason the feud between the two families has been eliminated (and replaced with the far more relevant issue of date rape). Without Romeo (Rome), Benvolio (Ben Volaire) and Mercutio (Murray Q) become minor characters, although Murray Q is still linked to Ty Katz's death.

4. The character of Diane helps explain why Pierce is willing to wait for Julia, despite their age difference. Her prophecy replaces the role of the stars/fate in Shakespeare's original.

5. Shae K. Speare sounds like Shakespeare, who deals with issues arising from love, loss, jealousy and guilt(Note Shakespeare was married to Anne Hathaway; Speare is married to Andy, and like Shakespeare has twins, Judith and Hampton (Hamnet)

6. Shakespeare works for Global Health, whose benefactor is James Tudor

7.

	Act	Scene	Lines
One			
a.	1	1	179
b.	4	3	33

c.	1	Chorus	2
d.	1	2	85
e.	2	2	14
f.	3	1	57-58
Two			
	2	3	1
Three			
	4	1	12
Four			
	2	2	83-84
Five			
	2	2	174
Seven			
	2	2	34
	4	5	55
Nine			
	1	4	98
Ten			
	1	2	55-56
Eleven			
a.	1	5	45-50
b.	1	2	14
c.	2	2	86-87
d.	2	2	43-44
Twelve			
	3	4	29

Thirteen			
a.	1	5	111
b.	2	6	8
c.	1	2	26-30
d.	2	2	178-183
Fourteen			
	1	3	18-20, 39-40, 60
Fifteen			
a.	3	2	86-88
b.	3	5	221
c.	1	3	13
d.	3	2	28-31
e.	1	3	12-13
f.	2	4	14
Sixteen			
	4	5	6-7
Seventeen			
a.	4	3	15
b.	3	3	110
c.	3	5	6
Eighteen			
a.	1	2	8
b.	1	Chorus	7
Nineteen			
a.	4	3	30-32
b.	4	3	50
c.	4	1	105

Twenty			
a.	1	4	22
b.	5	3	111
c.	2	2	90-93
d.	3	5	170
e.	2	3	58
f.	2	2	147-148
g.	5	1	1-3
h.	5	3	114-115
i.	3	2	20-22
Twenty Two			
	3	5	220
Twenty-three			
a.	1	5	122-123
b.	2	2	140-141
c.	2	2	26
d.	3	5	232
e.	1	3	81-86

I have also tried to maintain a symbiotic relationship between the two pieces in the chapters where Pierce and Loren Cappell discuss a potential marriage to Julia; the chapter with Pierce and Julia in the courtyard evokes the balcony scene; several times, Julia and Pierce are together at a dance, which is where Romeo and Juliet first met. Finally, Angelica's confusion when Julia appears at her apartment in Chapter Sixteen is an inversion of the situation in Act Three, Scene Two, where Juliet is confused by the nurse's incoherent explanation of Tybalt's death.